Heir Of The Fallen Crown

Art Vulcan

.

Published by Art Vulcan, 2024.

This is a work of fiction. Similarities to real people, places, or events are entirely coincidental.

HEIR OF THE FALLEN CROWN

First edition. October 7, 2024.

Copyright © 2024 Art Vulcan.

ISBN: 979-8227850515

Written by Art Vulcan.

Table of Contents

Chapter 1: 1
Chapter 2: 7
Chapter 3: 13
Chapter 4: 17
Chapter 5: 22
Chapter 6: 26
Chapter 7: 31
Chapter 8: 35
Chapter 9: 42
Chapter 10: 46
Chapter 11: 53
Chapter 12: 57
Chapter 13: 62
Chapter 14: 68
Chapter 15: 73
Chapter 16: 79
Chapter 17: 86
Chapter 18: 91
Chapter 19: 98
Chapter 20: 105

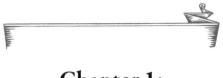

Chapter 1:

In the heart of Estonia's grand castle, a young boy named Aidan sat in a courtyard filled with the soft rustle of leaves and the occasional chirp of a distant bird. The castle's ancient stones, kissed by centuries of rain and baked by countless summers, whispered secrets of old as the shadows danced playfully across the cobblestone floor. Aidan, with his mop of unruly hair and eyes as blue as the midday sky, looked like any other child. But there was something distinctly royal about his posture, the way his small hands curled around the edges of his velvet tunic, and the quiet confidence in his stride. He was, after all, the prince of this land.

Across from him, with a scowl that could make even the strongest knight quake, stood his sister, Elena. Two years his senior, she had a fiery spirit and raven black hair, Her eyes, the same shade of blue as Aidan's, sparkled with indignation as she glared at him. Her hands were planted firmly on her hips, and the crunch of pebbles under her boots echoed through the courtyard as she approached. "You're such a brat," she spat out, her voice carrying the weight of a thousand disappointments.

Aidan smirked, his eyes dancing with mischief. "You're just mad because I outsmarted you," he said, his words carrying the delight of a victory won. He knew that his sister had always been the more serious one, the one who took her responsibilities as a future queen to heart. Her anger was like a storm, quick to form and fierce, while his was more like a spring shower—quick and gone.

Elena's cheeks flushed with a mix of embarrassment and anger. The prank Aidan had played on her was a simple one—switching the labels on her favorite herbs in the castle garden, leading her to make a concoction that ended up being a foul-smelling mess instead of a delightful perfume. It had been the talk of the castle for days, and she had been the butt of the joke more times than she cared to admit.

"Outsmarted? You call ruining hours of work 'smart'?" she retorted, her voice rising with each word. The courtyard, usually a place of peaceful solitude, now reverberated with their heated exchange. The castle staff, peeking from the windows and archways, exchanged knowing glances. Sibling rivalry in the royal family was nothing new. Gloria the 12 year old maid and friend to princess Elena was used to the young royals daily squabble to know ... It always got messy. She ducked a mudball thrown by Aidan with practiced ease as she rolled her eyes at her friend's antics.

Their voices grew louder, their words sharper, as they stood toe to toe. Aidan's smirk morphed into a full-blown grin, his teeth flashing in the sunlight. "It was just a bit of fun, Elena," he said, trying to sound nonchalant despite the sting of her words. But Elena was not easily appeased. Her eyes narrowed and she took a step closer, her voice low and dangerous.

"You think it's funny to make me look like a fool?" she hissed. Aidan felt a twinge of guilt, but his pride was too stubborn to let him admit it. He shrugged and leaned back on his hands, which were propped behind him on the cold stone bench. "In my experience you don't need any help looking like a fool" he said, his tone teasing.

Elena's eyes flashed, and for a moment, Aidan thought she might actually hit him. But before she could act on her fury, a firm voice echoed through the courtyard, cutting through the tension like a hot knife through butter. "Prince Aidan, Princess Elena, your presence is requested in the throne room immediately."

The siblings froze, their eyes darting to the source of the interruption. It was Sir Marcus, their father's most trusted advisor, his stern gaze boring into them from the archway that led to the castle's main corridor. Aidan felt his heart sink. He knew that look—it meant trouble.

Their fight forgotten for the moment, the two of them exchanged glances of apprehension. They had been summoned to the throne room before, but it was rarely for something good. The air grew heavier, the playfulness of their earlier argument replaced by a palpable tension that seemed to cling to the very air around them.

They straightened their clothes and took deep breaths to compose themselves, trying to look as regal as they could muster under the circumstances.

Sir Marcus looked displeased, his eyes flicking between the two of them as they approached. His expression was a clear indication that he had witnessed their squabble and disapproved. He turned on his heel and led the way through the archway without saying a word, expecting them to follow in silence. The cobblestone path beneath their feet grew more daunting with each step, the echoes of their footsteps seemingly bouncing off the towering stone walls, amplifying their anxiety.

As they entered the grand throne room, the heavy oak doors creaked shut behind them, emphasizing the gravity of the situation. The room was vast, with tall, stained-glass windows casting a kaleidoscope of colors on the gleaming marble floor. The throne itself was an imposing sight, made of the finest mahogany and adorned with gold leaf, standing on a raised dais at the far end. Their father, King Ulric, sat upon it, his expression a blend of disappointment and concern.

"What did I tell you two about fighting?" he asked, his voice deep and resonant. The room seemed to shrink around Aidan and Elena, making them feel like the smallest creatures in the kingdom.

They both swallowed hard, avoiding eye contact with their father. It was a question they had heard countless times before, one that usually preluded a lecture about their royal duties and the importance of setting an example.

"We know, Father," Elena said, her voice small. Aidan nodded in agreement, his cheeks reddening.

"Then why do I find you bickering in the courtyard for all to see?" King Ulric's eyes searched theirs, looking for understanding, perhaps even a hint of regret.

Aidan and Elena exchanged a sheepish glance. They knew their father's words were more than just a scolding; they were a gentle reminder of the weight of their titles and the responsibilities that came with it. "It just happened, Father," Aidan muttered, his voice barely audible.

King Ulric sighed, his gaze softening. "I understand that you're children and that sibling rivalry is inevitable," he said, his voice tinged with a hint of sadness. "But you must learn to control your emotions, especially in public. The people of Estonia look up to you both as their future rulers. They need to see strength and unity, not petty squabbles."

Both Aidan and Elena muttered their apologies, their heads bowed in shame. They knew their father was right—their actions reflected poorly on the monarchy. The weight of their titles settled heavily on their young shoulders as they made their way back to their chambers, the echo of their footsteps a constant reminder of their responsibilities.

Elena shot Aidan a glare that could freeze fire. "This is all your fault," she whispered through gritted teeth as they ascended the grand staircase, its crimson carpet muffling their steps. "You and your stupid pranks."

Aidan bit his tongue, knowing better than to argue with her in their current state. He offered a sheepish smile instead. "Maybe it's for the best," he murmured. "It'll give us a break from each other."

Elena rolled her eyes, but the corners of her mouth twitched upward slightly. Despite their rivalry, there was an undeniable bond between the two—one that had been forged in countless shared moments of joy, fear, and sorrow. They had always had each other's backs, even when they were at each other's throats.

Aidan was indeed a prodigy in the art of combat. At the tender age of ten, he had bested knights twice his age in mock battles, his reflexes and strategic thinking unmatched. His passion for the craft had earned him the title "The Young Lion," a nod to both his fiery spirit and the royal crest that adorned their family's banners. Yet, it was not just his physical prowess that set him apart; it was his maturity and intelligence that truly made him a formidable opponent. He studied the art of war and diplomacy as if it were a game of chess, always thinking five moves ahead.

Elena, on the other hand, had her own set of skills. While Aidan was out training with the knights, she could often be found poring over ancient tomes in the castle's vast library. Her mind was a sponge, soaking up knowledge of history, politics, and the subtle art of ruling a kingdom. Her wisdom was like a beacon, drawing advisors to seek her counsel despite her youth.

The siblings were a perfect balance, each complementing the other's strengths and weaknesses. Yet, their rivalry remained as fierce as ever. It was as if the very air between them crackled with energy, a constant reminder of the competition that fueled their growth. Their squabbles were legendary among the castle staff, who often found themselves caught in the crossfire of their wit and sarcasm.

Chapter 2:

The next morning, the castle awoke to the sound of a distant trumpet, signaling the arrival of an important guest. The courtyard buzzed with activity as knights and servants alike prepared to welcome the envoy from the neighboring kingdom of Lotharia. The air was charged with excitement and anticipation—a treaty was to be discussed, and the fate of the two lands hung in the balance.

The man who stepped from the carriage was tall and lean, with a sharp jawline and piercing eyes that missed nothing. He was Count Aldric, Lotharia's most skilled diplomat and a man whose words could slice through steel. He was flanked by a contingent of his own guards, all dressed in the deep purple and silver of their country's colors. Their armor gleamed in the early light, a stark contrast to the more subdued tones of Estonian steel.

The count's arrival had been announced with the grandeur befitting his station, the trumpets echoing through the castle corridors. The siblings, still nursing bruised egos from the previous day's argument, were ushered into the grand receiving hall, where they were to stand by their father's side as the envoy was greeted. Elena had spent hours perfecting her royal demeanor, her eyes focused and her back ramrod straight.

Aidan, on the other hand, fidgeted nervously, his mind racing with thoughts of swords and battles rather than treaties and alliances.

Count Aldric's gaze swept over the assembly, pausing briefly on Elena before settling on Aidan. "The Young Lion, I presume?" he said, a knowing smile playing on his lips. Aidan felt his cheeks flush under the scrutiny. He had heard whispers of the count's reputation—his sharp wit and shrewd negotiating skills were the stuff of legend.

King Ulric stepped forward, extending his hand in greeting. "Welcome, Count Aldric," he said warmly. "We are honored by your presence." The count took the king's hand, his grip firm and sure. His eyes never left Aidan's, as if sizing him up, testing his mettle from afar.

The treaty negotiations began with an elaborate banquet, the likes of which had not been seen in Estonia for years. The air was thick with the scent of roasting meats and exotic spices, the clink of silverware against fine china creating a symphony of sound. The great hall buzzed with the chatter of lords and ladies, their voices a cacophony of excitement and intrigue.

But amidst the pomp and circumstance, Aidan couldn't shake the feeling that Count Aldric was not all that he seemed. His smile was too wide, his eyes too knowing. Every time the count's gaze swept over the room, it lingered just a bit too long on the castle's defenses, the strategic placements of the knights, and the royal family's expressions. It was as if he was cataloging the kingdom's vulnerabilities, preparing for a battle of words rather than one of swords.

The banquet table groaned under the weight of the feast—platters of roast swan, steaming lobster, and exotic fruits from across the sea. The adults spoke in hushed tones, their eyes gleaming with the promise of wealth and power. But the air was taut with tension, like the string of a bow drawn too tightly. Aidan picked at his food, his appetite lost amidst his unease. He knew his sister felt it too—Elena's eyes darted to him every few moments, seeking reassurance that he shared her suspicion.

Count Aldric spoke with a silver tongue, weaving a tapestry of friendship and mutual benefit. Yet, Aidan couldn't shake the feeling that the count's words were as false as a serpent's smile. His eyes kept straying to the Lotharian guards, their arms folded and stoic expressions unmoving. They were a stark reminder of the power play unfolding before them.

During the feast, Aidan's eyes never left the count. Every gesture, every word, was meticulously studied. The way Aldric's eyes flickered to the castle's exits, the way his hand hovered just a tad too long over his own dagger—it all screamed 'trouble' and not the good kind. The prince's gut was a knot of unease, his senses heightened like a hawk scanning the fields for a hidden foe.

Elena, too, noticed the subtle signs of tension. She watched as her brother's shoulders grew tight, his eyes narrowing as he scrutinized their guest. She knew Aidan's instincts were rarely wrong, and she couldn't help but feel a shiver of concern. The two shared a look, a silent promise to be vigilant. They had been taught to trust their intuition, a lesson their father had drilled into them from an early age.

The count's speech grew more grandiose as the night progressed, his words painting a picture of an alliance that would make both kingdoms unstoppable. Yet, with each toast to friendship and prosperity, Aidan's unease grew stronger. There was something about the way Count Aldric's hand lingered on the pommel of his sword, something about the way his smile never quite reached his eyes, that set the prince's nerves on edge.

Elena's mind raced. If they were to voice their concerns to their father without solid evidence, it would only serve to fuel the king's frustration with Aidan's incessant need for caution. They had to be smart, to find a way to uncover the truth without betraying their own suspicions.

As the night went on, Aidan and Elena exchanged knowing glances, their thoughts in perfect harmony. They were the king's eyes and ears, and it was their duty to protect their kingdom from any threat, no matter how well-disguised. They had to be as subtle as shadows, as silent as the night, to unravel the count's true intentions.

Aidan took a page from Elena's book, using his charm to weave his way through the banquet guests. His curiosity led him to the castle's map room, where he hoped to find some clue to the count's plan. The room was dimly lit, the flicker of candles casting eerie shadows on the ancient parchments that lined the walls. His heart pounded in his chest as he approached a large table dominated by an intricate map of the lands.

As he studied the map, his eyes fell upon something peculiar—a tiny piece of parchment sticking out from beneath the heavy tome of alliances. His pulse quickened as he gently pulled it free, unfurling the paper with trembling hands. It was a sketch of Estonian defenses, annotated with precise, military-like notes in an unfamiliar hand. The realization struck him like a bolt of lightning—Count Aldric was planning an invasion!

Elena, meanwhile, had been listening intently to the conversations around her, her sharp mind picking up on the subtle nuances that most would miss. She overheard whispers of Lotharia's growing military might and the count's insatiable hunger for power. Her stomach twisted into knots as she pieced together the puzzle, her suspicion of the envoy growing stronger by the minute.

The siblings met back in the safety of their shared chamber, the heavy oak door shut firmly behind them. They exchanged their findings in hushed tones, their faces a mirror of each other's concern. "We must inform Father," Elena said urgently, her voice barely a whisper.

They found King Ulric in his study, the room suffused with the warm glow of candlelight and the scent of aged leather and parchment. The king looked up from his paperwork, his expression expectant. "What is it, children?" he asked, his eyes weary from the long day of preparations.

Aidan took a deep breath, the parchment trembling in his hand. "Father, I believe Count Aldric is not here for a treaty," he began, his voice wavering slightly. "I found this in the map room—it's a sketch of our defenses."

King Ulric looked up from his scrolls, raising an eyebrow. "A sketch, you say?" He took the parchment from Aidan's hand and studied it with a critical eye.

Elena nodded fervently, her voice filled with urgency. "And I've heard whispers, Father. The count's interest in our lands is more than just diplomatic."

King Ulric sighed and set the parchment down, his gaze weary. "Aidan, Elena, your imaginations are running wild," he said gently. "Count Aldric is an esteemed guest. He is here to discuss an alliance that could bring peace and prosperity to both our lands."

The siblings exchanged disbelieving looks. Aidan's fists clenched at his sides. "But Father, you have to believe us!" he insisted, his voice rising. "The evidence is right here!"

Elena placed a calming hand on her brother's shoulder. "Please, Father, we're not making this up. The count's actions, his interest in our defenses—it all points to something more nefarious."

But King Ulric was unyielding. "Your suspicions are unfounded," he said, his tone firm. "We have been preparing for this alliance for months. I trust Count Aldric."

Elena and Aidan left the study feeling both frustrated and confused. Why wasn't their father taking their warnings seriously? They had always been able to rely on his keen instincts, his unyielding sense of duty to their kingdom. Was he blinded by the allure of power and wealth?

Chapter 3:

Elena took Aidan's hand, her grip firm and reassuring. "We can't just sit back and do nothing," she whispered fiercely. "We need to find a way to prove our suspicions."

Aidan nodded, his eyes gleaming with determination. "We'll have to be clever," he said. "We can't just go to Father with our fears again. He'll think we're paranoid."

They decided to investigate further on their own, using their unique skills to uncover the truth. Aidan would focus on the castle's defenses and any signs of a potential Lotharian infiltration, while Elena would delve deeper into the political motives behind the treaty. They agreed to meet back in their chamber before dawn to share their findings.

Elena retreated to her part of the castle, her mind racing. She had always been her father's confidant, the one he turned to for counsel and wisdom beyond her years. His dismissal of their suspicions was a blow to her confidence, but she knew she couldn't let that deter her. Her heart was in her throat as she slipped into the shadowy corridors, her soft footsteps echoing against the stone. She knew every nook and cranny of the castle, and she was determined to find something that would prove their fears were not unfounded.

Aidan, on the other hand, found his way to the training grounds, his thoughts as sharp as the sword he picked up from the rack. He had always felt a bit of a strain in his relationship with the king—his father had always pushed him harder than Elena, expecting greatness from the day he could hold a toy sword.

He remembered the first time he'd bested Sir Marcus in a spar. He'd been just six, and his heart had raced with excitement as he looked to his father for approval. But the king's expression had remained stoic, his eyes cold. "It's not enough," he'd said, turning away to speak with advisors. Aidan had felt a flicker of anger, a flame that had fueled his training ever since.

By the time he was seven, Aidan had surpassed even the most skilled knights. Yet, the praise he craved remained elusive. So he'd turned to the younger squires, eager to pass on his knowledge. He'd seen their eyes light up with the same excitement he'd once felt, watched them grow into formidable warriors under his tutelage. But the warmth of their admiration was a poor substitute for his father's praise.

The siblings had always known that King Ulric's expectations were high, but Aidan had never felt the coldness of his dismissal so acutely. As the heir to the throne, he'd been groomed to be the embodiment of Estonian might—his every move scrutinized, his every victory celebrated. But now, when it truly mattered, his father's faith in him was as absent as the warmth of the sun in winter.

Elena's thoughts mirrored Aidan's as she wandered through the castle's labyrinthine halls. The echoes of their footsteps seemed to mock their shared inadequacy. Yet, she couldn't help but feel a twinge of anger. It wasn't just about the rejection; it was about the future of their kingdom. If their father couldn't see the danger in Count Aldric's smile, then it was up to them to save Estonia.

Meanwhile, unbeknownst to them, Count Aldric had indeed become aware of their suspicions. The whispers of the castle walls had carried their concerns to his sharp ears, and he knew that the prince and princess could not be allowed to interfere. His plan was simple—to discredit Aidan, the more vocal of the two, and to isolate Elena.

In the dead of night, he approached the king with a grave expression. "Your majesty," he began, his voice a serpent's hiss in the quiet chamber. "I have uncovered a grave betrayal within your own walls."

King Ulric looked up, his eyes narrowing. "What betrayal, Count?"

Aldric paused for dramatic effect. "Your son, Aidan. He has been consorting with the very forces you have outlawed—magic."

The king's eyes widened in disbelief, his hand tightening around the goblet of wine he held. "What proof do you have of this treachery?"

Count Aldric produced a small, ornate box, its surface inlaid with a swirl of precious stones that gleamed eerily in the candlelight. He opened it with a dramatic flourish to reveal a handful of shimmering dust. "This," he said, his voice low and menacing, "was found in the prince's chamber. It is the residue of a dark incantation, one that could only be performed by someone in league with the forbidden arts."

King Ulric's face paled, his grip on the goblet turning white-knuckled. Magic had been outlawed in Estonia for decades, the mere mention of it enough to incite fear and revulsion. To think that his own son could be involved with such heresy... It was unthinkable. Yet, the evidence was laid before him, a glittering betrayal that seemed to dance in the flickering shadows.

Aidan had always had a rebellious streak, pushing the boundaries of what was expected of a future king. But consorting with magic? It was a line that could never be crossed, a truth that had been etched into the very fabric of their kingdom's laws. The king's mind reeled, trying to reconcile the image of his son with the gravity of the accusation.

Without another word, King Ulric nodded to the count. "Summon the knights," he said, his voice a cold whisper. "We will deal with this treachery swiftly."

Elena and Aidan had no idea of the plot unfolding against them. They were too busy sneaking through the castle, driven by their own sense of duty and the need to protect their home. As Elena delicately picked through the royal archives, her eyes scanning over dusty scrolls and ancient tomes, she couldn't help but feel a growing unease. Her father had always taught them that loyalty to the crown came first, but now it seemed as if that very loyalty was being questioned.

Chapter 4:

In the training yard, Aidan's blade sang through the night air, his movements a dance of shadows and steel. He knew every nook and cranny of the castle defenses, every secret passage and potential weakness. Yet, he couldn't shake the feeling that he was searching for a ghost—his father's trust. It was as elusive as the wind, and just as unpredictable.

As he practiced, his thoughts grew darker. What if Elena and he were wrong? What if they were just seeing shadows where there were none? But then he thought of the sketch, the way the count's eyes had lingered on the castle's defenses, and he knew they weren't.

Suddenly, the night air was pierced by the sound of marching boots. Aidan's heart leaped to his throat as he saw a contingent of guards approaching the training grounds, their torches casting flickering shadows on the walls. His instincts screamed at him to flee, but his loyalty to his father and his kingdom held him firm.

The guards, faces grim and unwavering, marched closer. "Prince Aidan," their captain called out, his voice firm. "You are under arrest by order of the king."

Aidan's heart sank. This couldn't be happening. "What is the charge?" he demanded, though he knew the answer. The glittering dust, the lies of Count Aldric—it all fell into place. He sheathed his sword, his hands trembling with a mix of anger and fear.

The captain stepped forward, his eyes filled with regret. "Your Highness," he said, his voice tight, "you are charged with treason—conspiring with the forbidden arts." Aidan could see the doubt in the man's eyes, the loyalty to his king warring with his own suspicion. But the guard had his orders, and he was bound to follow them.

The world seemed to tilt on its axis as the reality of the situation sank in. His father had believed the count's lies, and now he was to be punished for a crime he had not committed. The guards approached, their expressions a mix of determination and trepidation. He knew they had no choice but to obey the king's command, yet he couldn't help but feel a surge of anger and betrayal.

But just as Aidan was about to be taken away, a figure emerged from the shadows, her cloak billowing like the wings of an avenging angel. It was Elena. Her eyes were wide with shock and fear, and she sprinted towards him, her hand reaching for his. "Aidan," she gasped. "What is happening?"

The guards halted, their eyes flicking to the princess before returning to the prince. "Your Highness," the captain said, his tone now laced with caution. "Your father, the king, has ordered your brother's arrest."

Elena's heart hammered in her chest. "What? On what grounds?" she demanded, her voice shaking with fear. The captain looked to Aidan, his gaze apologetic.

"For consorting with magic, Highness," he replied gravely. "We found evidence in his chamber."

Elena's mind reeled. Magic? That was impossible—Aidan knew the consequences of such treason. She searched her brother's face, desperate for a sign of understanding, but his expression was a storm of confusion and anger.

"Father can't truly believe this," she whispered, her voice barely audible above the thunder of her own heart. "We have to talk to him."

But the guards didn't waver, their swords at the ready. "Princess," the captain said gently, "you must stand down. The king's word is law."

Elena's eyes narrowed. "Law is meant to protect, not to deceive," she spat, her voice as sharp as a rapier. "Count Aldric has played you for fools. This is a setup, a ploy to divide us!"

The captain looked uncomfortable, his eyes flicking to the other guards. "We have no choice, Your Highness," he said gruffly. "We must bring the prince to the dungeons for questioning."

Aidan stepped closer to Elena, his eyes never leaving the captain's. "It'll be fine, Elena," he murmured, trying to infuse his voice with a confidence he didn't feel. "I'll explain everything to Father. You just need to keep an eye on things here."

Elena knew the mask he wore was a façade—his jaw was clenched tight, his eyes filled with a rage she had rarely seen. But she also knew her brother; he was trying to be brave for her. He was trying to ease her fears, to make her believe that somehow, this would all be resolved.

But she remembered the other times—the whispers of his punishments that had echoed through the castle halls, the days of his absence that had turned into weeks. The bruises that had once lined his back when she had managed to sneak into the dungeons with a tray of food and a soothing balm. The way their father had looked away, ashamed of his own actions, when Aidan had finally emerged, head held high despite his pain.

Elena knew that dungeon's chilling embrace all too well—the dampness that clung to your skin, the scent of despair that lingered in the air. She had seen it etched into her brother's eyes every time he returned from his father's "lessons." And she knew that this time, with the stakes so high, the consequences would be severe.

The captain's gaze softened, and she could see the doubt in his eyes. Perhaps he had witnessed Aidan's previous returns, too, and knew the truth behind the king's "disciplinary measures." Perhaps he had a son of his own, and the thought of such treatment made his stomach turn.

Elena took a deep breath, her mind racing. She knew she had to act fast. "I will go with him," she declared firmly. "I will not leave my brother's side while these baseless accusations are thrown at him."

The captain hesitated, his gaze flickering between the siblings. "Your Highness, it is not protocol for a member of the royal family to accompany a prisoner to the dungeons," he said, his voice strained.

But Elena was undeterred. "I will not leave Aidan's side," she said, her voice firm. "I know what happens in those dank cells, and I will not stand by while he is punished for a crime he did not commit."

Aidan looked at his sister, his heart heavy. He knew her resolve was unshakeable, but the thought of her in such a place, the dungeons that had held him captive too many times to count, was unbearable. He took her hands in his, his eyes pleading. "Elena, please. If Father sees you defying him now, it will only make things worse."

Elena's gaze was steely, her jaw set. "Aidan, we are in this together," she said firmly. "If Father won't listen to you, maybe he'll listen to me."

Aidan felt a twinge of doubt, but he also knew his sister's power of persuasion. In the past, she had been able to coax their father's softer side to the forefront, turning his coldness into a gentle warmth. But these last few months had been different. The king had become more distant, his eyes harder, his words sharper. Aidan couldn't bear the thought of her facing that side of their father.

"Elena," he said softly, "I don't think Father will listen to you now. He's... changed."

Elena searched her brother's eyes, the depths of his fear and frustration resonating with her own. She knew Aidan was right—their father had become a different man in recent months. His once warm smile had been replaced with a stern glare, his patience with Aidan's rebellious spirit wearing ever thinner.

Finally, with a sigh that seemed to carry the weight of the castle's stones, she nodded. "Very well," she whispered, her voice tight with emotion. "But I will not rest until I've uncovered the truth and proven your innocence."

The guards stepped forward, their expressions a mix of sympathy and resolve. They took Aidan firmly by the arms and led him away, his footsteps echoing through the cold, damp corridors of the castle's bowels. Elena watched him go, her heart aching with each step he took away from her. She knew she had to be strong, for both of them.

Chapter 5:

The dungeons were a place of darkness and despair, the very embodiment of fear. Aidan had been there before, but this time was different. This time, it was not for his own rebellious actions but for a lie concocted by a snake in their midst. As they descended the stone steps, the air grew heavier, the scent of mold and misery thickening with each step. The flickering torchlight cast eerie shadows that danced along the walls, whispering of the castle's forgotten secrets and the souls that had suffered within these very walls.

The guards' grip on Aidan's arms was firm but not brutal, a silent acknowledgment of their shared discomfort. They were men of honor, forced to act on the king's command, and the weight of that duty etched lines of conflict on their faces. The clank of iron bars and the distant cries of the imprisoned seemed to resonate with the rhythm of his racing heart.

In the dungeon's dimly lit chamber, the air was thick with the scent of fear and the cold, clammy touch of damp stone. King Ulric stood there, his silhouette cast long and imposing by the flickering torchlight. Aidan felt a lump form in his throat as he was brought before his father. The king's face was a mask of disappointment, a stark contrast to the warmth that once filled his eyes whenever he looked upon his son.

"Your Royal Highness," the guard captain announced, his voice echoing off the damp walls.

King Ulric stepped forward, the torchlight playing across the harsh lines of his face. His eyes, once warm with pride, were now cold and accusatory as they fell upon Aidan. "Son," he began, his voice a sad rumble that seemed to shake the very foundations of the chamber.

Aidan's knees felt like water, but he held his father's gaze, his own eyes flashing with a mix of anger and defiance. "Father," he said, his voice clear and strong despite his fear.

King Ulric's eyes searched his son's face, looking for any sign of the treachery he had been led to believe. "What do you have to say for yourself?" he asked, his voice heavy with sadness.

Aidan took a deep, steadying breath. "I am innocent of the charges laid against me," he declared, his voice echoing in the dank chamber. "I have not consorted with magic. This is a lie, a ploy by Count Aldric to turn you against me and destabilize our kingdom."

The king's expression remained unchanged, his eyes as cold as the stone around them. "The evidence speaks for itself," he said, his voice a chilling echo in the silent space.

But Aidan's resolve did not waver. "The evidence has been planted," he insisted, his voice strong despite the fear that clutched at his throat. "You know me, Father. You know I would never betray you, never betray Estonia."

King Ulric's hand shot out like lightning, his palm connecting with Aidan's cheek with a resounding crack. The prince stumbled backwards, the taste of copper flooding his mouth. He was used to his father's physical punishments—the beatings that were meant to shape him into the king he was destined to become. But this was different. This was not a punishment for a misdeed, but for a crime he hadn't committed. The pain in his cheek was a stark reminder of the chasm that had opened between them.

Elena watched, her eyes wide with shock, as her brother's head snapped to the side. The sight of their father's hand raised against Aidan was like a dagger in her heart, and she had to fight the urge to rush forward and protect him. But she knew it would only make things worse. Instead, she took a step back, her hands balled into fists at her sides.

"Father," she said, her voice trembling with a mix of anger and fear. "You must listen to Aidan. This is not him."

King Ulric's eyes snapped to hers, the coldness in them deepening. "Silence," he barked. "You will not speak unless spoken to."

Elena felt a chill run through her veins, but she remained steadfast. "Father," she said, her voice firm despite the tremor in her chest. "You are making a grave mistake."

King Ulric's gaze bore into her, his eyes like chips of ice. "Guards," he said, his voice devoid of emotion, "return the princess to her chambers. She is not to leave until I say so."

Elena felt a surge of panic, but she knew better than to argue. With one last, pleading look at Aidan, she allowed herself to be escorted out of the dungeon, her thoughts racing. How could her father be so blind? How could he believe such a vile lie? Her mind was a whirlwind of questions and fear for her brother's fate.

The guards led her back through the castle's shadowy halls, their footsteps echoing like a funeral procession. She could feel their eyes on her, filled with a mix of pity and loyalty to the crown. They knew her, knew her kindness and her intelligence. They knew Aidan, too, and she could see the doubt in their gazes.

When they reached her chamber, the guards stepped aside to allow her to enter, but Elena had other plans. "Leave us," she ordered, her voice firm despite the tremble in her hands. The guards hesitated for a moment before bowing and retreating, closing the heavy oak door behind them with a thud that seemed to echo through the corridor.

With trembling fingers, Elena reached for the latch on her window, the only source of fresh air in the stifling room. The cool night breeze was a welcome respite from the thick tension that had settled over her. Her thoughts raced as she looked out over the moonlit courtyard, her mind searching for a way to save Aidan. The king had never been one to act hastily, but the coldness in his voice, the unwavering conviction in his eyes—it was as if he had become a stranger overnight.

In the dungeons below, Aidan felt the cold steel of the damp cell walls against his back as the guards secured his wrists with shackles. The clank of the iron bars echoed in the silent chamber, a mournful song of despair. The king had not even allowed him a trial, so certain was he of Aidan's guilt. It was a fate worse than death, to be condemned without a chance to defend oneself, especially by the very man who was supposed to believe in him the most.

King Ulric's eyes bore into him, the warmth that once shone there now extinguished, leaving only the cold, hard gleam of accusation. "You will be executed at dawn," he said, his voice as emotionless as the stones that surrounded them. "Your treachery will not be tolerated in this kingdom."

Chapter 6:

Aidan felt the blood drain from his face, his heart racing like a wild steed in his chest. Execution? For a crime he hadn't committed? The very thought was a nightmare made real, a fate he never could have imagined for himself. "Father, please," he choked out, desperation tingeing his words. "I am your son. You must believe me."

But King Ulric's expression remained as unyielding as the very stones of the castle. "I am king first, and your father second," he said, his voice echoing off the cold walls of the dungeon. "I will not allow treachery to go unpunished, even if it is by my own flesh and blood."

The words hit Aidan like a blow to the chest, knocking the wind from his lungs. Execution? At dawn? He couldn't believe what he was hearing. He searched his father's eyes for any sign of mercy, any spark of the love he knew was buried deep within the man who had raised him. But all he found was a cold, hard stare that sent shivers down his spine.

As King Ulric turned away, the heavy thud of his footsteps reverberating through the dungeon, Aidan's mind raced. He had to escape, had to prove his innocence. The shackles bit into his wrists, a harsh reminder of his new reality. The bars of his cell slammed shut with a finality that seemed to suck the air from the room.

Above, in the castle's higher chambers, whispers of the shocking order spread like wildfire. Courtiers and servants alike spoke in hushed tones of the prince's treason, their faces a mix of fear and disbelief. The castle, once a bastion of warmth and joy, now felt like a prison of lies and deceit.

Meanwhile, in her chamber, Elena waited, her heart racing. The silence was deafening, the only sound the ticking of the clock, each second a mockery of the time that was slipping away from Aidan's grasp. Suddenly, the door burst open, and Gloria, her eyes wide with terror, rushed inside.

"Elena" she panted, her breath coming in short gasps. "It's Aidan... he's been... "

Elena's heart felt like it was going to shatter in her chest. "What happened?" she whispered, dreading the answer.

Gloria's eyes filled with tears. "They've taken him to the dungeons," she sobbed. "The king... he said... Aidan is to be executed at dawn."

Elena felt as though she had been struck by lightning. Execution? For something he hadn't done? It was impossible, a twisted nightmare she couldn't wake from. But she knew she had to be strong for her brother, for herself. She couldn't let the fear and anger consume her. She took a deep breath and turned to her friend, her voice firm. "We will not let this happen," she said. "We will find a way to save him."

The two girls huddled together, their hearts racing with the urgency of their mission. They had to act fast, before dawn's cruel light brought with it the executioner's blade. Gloria's eyes searched hers, looking for the strength she knew Elena had in abundance. "What can we do?" she whispered.

Elena took a deep breath, her mind racing. "We must find the evidence that proves Aidan's innocence," she said, her voice firm with determination. "Count Aldric is behind this. We know it."

Gloria nodded, her eyes shining with unshed tears. "But where do we start?" she asked. "The castle is vast, and the night is almost upon us."

Elena's gaze hardened, and she took a deep breath. "We start with the map room," she said decisively. "That's where we found the first clue. Maybe there's something we missed."

The two of them raced through the castle's corridors, their hearts pounding in unison with every step. The castle's grandeur seemed to close in on them, the opulent tapestries and gleaming suits of armor mocking the dire situation. They slipped past sleeping guards and patrols, their every move calculated to avoid detection. The night was their ally, cloaking them in shadows as they sought the truth that would save Aidan.

Elena's mind was a whirlwind of fear and anger. Her father had always been strict, but to accuse Aidan of treason and order his execution without a trial? It was unthinkable. Her thoughts kept returning to the conversation they had with King Ulric earlier, the doubt in the guards' eyes, the way the captain had hesitated. There was a crack in the façade, a hint that not everyone was convinced of Aidan's guilt.

Her eyes searched the map room, her gaze flickering over the detailed parchments and scrolls. The candlelight cast dancing shadows across the walls, and she felt the weight of the castle's secrets pressing down upon her. Gloria hovered nearby, her eyes darting nervously from corner to corner, her hand clutching the hilt of the small dagger hidden beneath her skirts.

Elena's mind raced, trying to piece together the puzzle that was their father's accusation. Why would Count Aldric go to such lengths to frame Aidan? What did he stand to gain from their father's distrust? The answers were there, hidden within the castle's storerooms and corridors, whispered by the very stones themselves.

Her eyes fell upon a small, seemingly innocuous scroll tucked in the corner of the room, partially obscured by a dusty tome. With trembling fingers, she pulled it free and unfurled it, revealing a set of complex symbols and incantations—the very essence of dark magic. Her heart skipped a beat. This was no child's trick or jest. This was the real McCoy, the kind of evidence that could convince even the most skeptical of kings.

"Gloria," she murmured, her voice tight with fear and anger. "Look at this."

Gloria stepped closer, her eyes widening as she took in the scroll. "Elena," she breathed, her voice hushed. "This is real dark magic."

Elena nodded, her heart racing. "We have to show this to Father," she said, her voice low and urgent. "He has to see that Aidan is innocent."

But Gloria's expression was troubled. "What if he doesn't believe us?" she whispered. "What if he's already made up his mind?"

Elena's jaw set with determination. "We have to try," she said. "Aidan's life is at stake. We cannot sit idly by."

With that, she handed the scroll to Gloria. "You go to him," she said, her voice low but firm. "Tell him we are working to clear his name. Give him hope. I will go to Father and present this evidence."

Gloria took the scroll with trembling hands, her eyes wide with fear but also determination. "I will not fail," she promised before slipping away into the shadows, her footsteps as light as a ghost's whisper.

Chapter 7:

Elena watched her go, her heart pounding like a war drum. She knew the path to the king's chamber, had walked it countless times in her dreams and nightmares. The corridors felt like they stretched on forever, the flickering candlelight playing tricks with her eyes. Her mind raced with the words she would say, the arguments she would present. But the coldness in her father's eyes haunted her, a specter that whispered doubt into her ears.

As she approached the royal chamber, she took a deep, steadying breath. She had to be the voice of reason, the beacon of truth in the sea of lies that had engulfed their once-happy kingdom. With a trembling hand, she pushed open the heavy oak door, the hinges groaning in protest.

Inside, she found King Ulric sitting on his throne, his eyes dark and stormy. He looked up as she entered, and for a moment, she saw the flicker of doubt in his gaze. But it was quickly extinguished, replaced by a steely resolve that sent a shiver down her spine.

"Elena," he said, his voice as cold as the stone walls that surrounded them. "You are to return to your chamber."

Elena's hand tightened around the scroll, the incriminating evidence she hoped would save Aidan. "Father," she began, her voice shaking with emotion, "I've found something you must see."

King Ulric's gaze was as cold as the stone walls of his chamber. He looked at her with a mix of weariness and anger. "Your brother has been charged with treason," he said, his voice flat. "There is no evidence that can change that."

Elena stepped forward, her hand trembling as she offered the scroll. "But, Father, this is real dark magic," she said, her voice shaking with urgency. "This is not something Aidan would do. He is innocent."

King Ulric's gaze remained unyielding, his eyes as cold as the steel of his crown. "Your loyalty to your brother is admirable, Elena," he said, his voice like the crack of a whip. "But it is misplaced."

Elena's hand trembled as she held out the scroll, her heart racing like a wild steed. "But Father," she protested, her voice cracking with emotion, "this is not the work of a child playing at being a mage. This is true dark magic, and Aidan would never—"

King Ulric's eyes narrowed, his jaw set like granite. "Silence," he barked, cutting her off mid-sentence. He took the scroll with a heavy sigh, his eyes scanning the arcane symbols with a practiced gaze. For a moment, the room was as quiet as a tomb, the only sound the distant toll of a midnight bell.

When he looked up, the coldness in his eyes had not abated. "This does not prove your brother's innocence, Elena," he said, his voice as cold as the steel that held Aidan captive below. "It only confirms that dark forces are at work within our walls."

Elena's heart sank. How could her father be so blind? The evidence lay right before him, the very symbols that would have sent any reasonable person racing to Aidan's side. But instead, he remained firm in his conviction, his eyes as unyielding as the bars that kept her brother from the world above.

"But Father," she insisted, her voice a desperate whisper, "this is not Aidan's handiwork. He would never dabble in such dark arts."

King Ulric's gaze was as unyielding as the castle's ancient stones. "Your loyalty is commendable, Elena," he said, his voice as cold as the steel of his crown. "But your judgment is clouded by your emotions. I have seen this before, in others who let their hearts lead them to ruin."

Elena felt a surge of anger and desperation, the injustice of it all burning in her chest like a wildfire. "But Father, why can't you see?" she pleaded, her voice trembling. "Aidan is innocent. This is Count Aldric's doing."

King Ulric's eyes flicked up from the scroll, his gaze piercing hers. "Count Aldric is a trusted advisor," he said, his voice like a wall of ice.

As if on cue, the doors to the chamber swung open, and the very man they were discussing strode in, his footsteps echoing through the cavernous space. Count Aldric's eyes swept over Elena with a smugness that made her skin crawl. His presence was like a dark cloud, casting a shadow over the room.

"Ah, the Wise Scholar," he said, his voice like oil on water. "I see you've found something of interest in your nocturnal wanderings."

Elena's grip tightened around the scroll, her knuckles white. "This is not a game, Count Aldric," she spat. "My brother's life is at stake."

The count's smile never wavered, his eyes glinting in the candlelight. "Ah, but it is precisely because of your emotions, Your Highness, that you are unable to see the truth," he purred, his voice a serpent's hiss. "The prince's own hand was found with these very incantations. How else could you explain it?"

Elena's mind raced, trying to piece together how Aldric had managed to frame Aidan so convincingly. "Father," she pleaded, "you must listen to me. This is a setup, a ploy to take control of Estonia."

But her words fell on deaf ears. King Ulric's gaze remained firmly on the scroll, his expression unchanged. It was as if she hadn't spoken at all. The silence grew heavier, pressing down on her like a suffocating blanket of despair.

Frustrated and on the brink of tears, Elena turned on her heel and stormed out of the chamber. As she retreated into the hallway, the weight of the castle's stones seemed to follow her, whispering of their ancient secrets. The flickering candlelight threw elongated shadows across the floor, and she could have sworn she saw Count Aldric's smug smile widen, even though his back was to her. The betrayal was palpable, a living entity that stung like a thousand wasps.

Chapter 8:

Elena's thoughts raced as she made her way back to the dungeons. The castle had become a prison for her too, its grandeur a mockery of the freedom she had once felt within its walls. The guards she passed eyed her with a mix of curiosity and wariness, but she kept her gaze firmly ahead, her steps swift and determined.

When she reached the dungeon, her heart was in her throat. The heavy door creaked open, and she descended the stairs into the cold, dank air. The clank of shackles and the distant sobs of the incarcerated echoed through the corridors, a symphony of despair that seemed to grow louder with every step she took towards Aidan's cell.

Elena's eyes searched the dimly lit corridor, finally settling on the familiar figure of her brother. Aidan's eyes lit up as he saw her, hope briefly piercing the darkness that had engulfed them both. "Elena," he called out, his voice hoarse from disuse. "What's happening?"

Her heart ached at the sight of him, shackled and defeated. "I've found something," she whispered urgently, her eyes darting around to ensure they weren't being watched. "But Father won't listen. He's convinced of your guilt."

Aidan's face fell, but he managed a weak smile. "It's okay, Elena," he said, his voice a mere thread of what it once was. "I knew it would be hard to convince him. But we can't give up hope."

Elena nodded, her eyes shining with determination. "We'll find another way," she assured him. "We have to."

Gloria, who had been quiet until now, spoke up, her voice a mix of fear and anger. "It's like the king can't see reason," she said, her words echoing in the cold dungeon. "It's as if he's blind to the truth right in front of him."

Aidan nodded solemnly, the gravity of the situation weighing heavily on his young shoulders. "We have to do something," he said, his eyes meeting Elena's with a silent plea. "We can't just sit here and wait for dawn."

Elena's gaze searched the damp stones of the dungeon, her mind racing. "We can't prove your innocence to Father," she murmured, "but we can escape."

Gloria's eyes lit up with hope. "How?" she asked, her voice barely above a whisper.

Aidan leaned closer, his voice dropping to a conspiratorial murmur. "The castle has a secret passage," he began, his eyes glinting with excitement. "A hidden way out, known only to a few."

Elena's heart leaped with hope. "Where is it?" she asked, her eyes searching her brother's face.

Back in the throne room, the count's persuasive words wove a deadly spell around the king's resolve. "Your daughter," Aldric said, his voice as smooth as velvet, "has proven to be as cunning as she is clever. If we do not act swiftly, she may succeed in her quest to free the traitor."

King Ulric's eyes narrowed, the flame of doubt flickering within them. "You speak the truth," he murmured, stroking his beard thoughtfully. "We cannot risk her meddling further in our affairs."

Count Aldric stepped closer, his smile cold and calculating. "If we act swiftly," he said, "we can eliminate the threat before it grows any stronger."

The king's booming voice echoed through the castle, the finality of his words a death knell in Elena's ears. "Bring the traitor to the executioner," he had said, and with that, Aidan's fate was sealed. A group of heavily armed guards marched towards the dungeon, their footsteps like a funeral procession.

Elena's heart raced as she heard the jangle of keys, the harsh metallic sound a grim reminder of the fate that awaited her brother. She looked at Aidan, his eyes reflecting the same fear and determination that she felt. "We have to go," she whispered, her voice trembling. "We can't let them take you."

The guards approached, their faces a mix of confusion and resolve. "Your Royal Highness," one said, his voice gruff but hesitant. "We have orders to bring the prince to the executioner."

Elena's eyes flashed with anger and defiance. "You will not take my brother," she spat, her voice echoing through the damp stones of the dungeon.

Aidan's gaze met hers, and in that instant, she saw the fierce strength that had earned him the nickname "The Young Lion." He stood tall, his shackles clanking as he straightened his shoulders. "I am not going anywhere with you," he said, his voice steady despite the fear that must have been coursing through his veins.

The guards exchanged glances, unsure how to proceed with the daughter of the king standing so boldly before them. "Your Highness," the leader began, his voice strained, "you must come with us."

Elena's eyes flashed, and she stepped in front of Aidan, her small frame blocking the path to the cell. "You will not pass," she said firmly, her voice ringing through the dungeon.

The guards paused, their expressions a mix of surprise and confusion. "Your Highness," their leader said, his voice wavering slightly. "We have our orders. You must not interfere."

Elena's eyes narrowed. "My place is with my brother," she said firmly. "I will not stand idly by while an innocent boy is thrown to his death."

The guards' expressions grew more uncertain, their eyes flicking between the determined siblings and the looming figure of king Ulric who had appeared at the top of the dungeon stairs. His face was a mask of fury, his eyes blazing with an intensity that sent a shiver down Elena's spine. "Guards," he boomed, his voice resonating through the dungeon, "remove the girl and proceed with the execution!"

The air grew thick with tension, the very stones of the castle seeming to hold their breath. Aidan's eyes never left hers, his gaze filled with a mix of fear, anger, and a fierce determination not to show it. They were outmatched, outmaneuvered, and their hearts hammered in their chests like the drums of a doomed battle but they fought with unmatched ferocity.

Despite the siblings strength and skill, the guards' numbers overwhelmed them. Elena and Aidan fought valiantly, their movements a blur of steel and fury. Swords clashed against shields, sparks flying in the dim light as they parried and thrust. The sound of battle filled the dungeon, a cacophony of grunts, steel on steel, and the occasional cry of pain.

Elena's slender blade darted and danced, a silver serpent weaving through the enemy's ranks, while Aidan's youthful strength sent men twice his size stumbling back. Yet, with each swing of their weapons, the reality of their situation grew clearer: they were two against many, and the castle's loyalty was not theirs to command. The guards, though hesitant, followed their king's orders, their eyes reflecting the conflict within their hearts.

The siblings' movements grew more desperate as the guard's numbers grew thicker, the air thick with the scent of sweat and fear. Each parry and thrust brought them closer to the brink of exhaustion, their breaths coming in ragged gasps. Despite their fierce spirit, the weight of the world seemed to bear down on them, their limbs growing heavier with every passing moment.

Elena's blade, once a gleaming beacon of hope, grew duller with each blocked blow, her arms trembling with fatigue. Aidan's youthful strength began to wane, his swings growing less powerful and precise. The guards, though clearly torn by their duty, pressed forward, their faces etched with grim determination. They had seen the king's wrath firsthand and knew the consequences of failure.

Aiden and Elena were pushed back, step by step, until their backs were against the cold, damp stones of the cell. The guards closed in, their swords a ring of steel around the siblings. Elena could feel the warmth of Aidan's breath on her neck as they fought side by side, their hearts pounding in unison. But the inevitable was closing in like the jaws of a great beast, and she knew that their end was near.

With a final, desperate lunge, she managed to disarm one of their attackers, but the victory was short-lived. A burly guard, his eyes filled with regret, grabbed her from behind, pinning her arms to her sides. Aiden roared in fury, throwing himself at the guard, but he was quickly subdued by a group of his comrades, their grip on him like iron.

Elena struggled and kicked, her eyes never leaving her brother's as the guards secured her own shackles. "Father!" she screamed up at the stairs, her voice raw with pain and betrayal. "Father, please!" But her cries fell on deaf ears, the king's silhouette retreating into the shadows above.

The guards, now in firm control, dragged Aidan away, his protests muffled by the gag they had hastily applied. Elena watched him go, her heart breaking with every step he took. "Elena," he called out to her, his eyes full of fear, but she knew he was trying to be strong, trying to tell her not to give up hope.

Her own captor had less empathy, his grip on her arms like a vice. "Your Highness," he said, his voice gruff with the weight of his duty, "you must come with us."

Elena's eyes remained locked on Aidan's retreating figure, her chest heaving with rage and despair. She knew that the guards were torn, that their hearts were not in this betrayal, but she had no words to ease their consciences. All she could do was fight, her spirit as unyielding as the ancient stones that surrounded them.

But as Aidan's cries grew fainter, she felt the world closing in around her, the very air thick with the scent of injustice. Several guards restrained her now, their grip unrelenting as they dragged her away from the cell, her legs kicking out wildly. Her eyes searched the shadows, seeking any hint of an escape or an ally, but the dungeon was a fortress of despair, offering no respite.

The procession of guards and the condemned prince grew louder as they ascended the winding stairs, the torches on the walls casting a flickering, hellish light upon their grim faces. Elena's heart felt as if it would burst from her chest, her eyes never leaving Aidan's as they approached the dreaded wall.

Chapter 9:

The guards were somber, their faces a canvas of conflicted emotions. Some avoided their gaze, others offered silent apologies, but none dared to oppose the king's command. Aidan's eyes searched hers for a sign of hope, a spark of a plan, but Elena had none to give.

As they reached the top of the stairs, the cold draft of the castle's highest tower met them, carrying the scent of rain and the promise of a bleak dawn. The guards shoved Aidan towards the parapet, the very edge of the castle walls, where the stone dropped away into the abyss below. His eyes were wide with fear, but his jaw remained set, a reflection of the fiery spirit that burned within.

Elena watched, her heart in her throat, as Aidan was forced to his knees. The guards stepped back, their faces a canvas of regret and resolve. One of them, the one who had shown the most hesitation, offered a silent, sorrowful nod to Aidan before turning away, unable to meet his gaze.

The executioner, a hulking figure with a cruel glint in his eye, stepped forward, His movements were efficient, practiced, and devoid of emotion—a stark contrast to the turmoil that raged within Elena's soul. She watched as Aidan's wrists were bound tightly, the coarse rope digging into his skin. He didn't struggle, didn't scream, didn't beg. He simply looked at her, his eyes a storm of emotions—fear, anger, love, and a fierce determination not to show his fear.

Elena felt her own anger boil over, a rage that burned like a supernova within her. With a strength born of desperation, she wrenched free of the guards' grasp, tearing away from their arms like a wild animal breaking from its chains. "Father!" she screamed, her voice a primal roar that echoed through the tower. "You cannot do this!"

Her eyes searched the shadows for any sign of the king, but he remained hidden, a coward behind his fortress of guards and false accusations. Her eyes found Aidan's again, his own filled with a resignation that broke her heart. He gave her a bittersweet smile, one that spoke volumes in its quiet dignity. It said he was ready to face his end, that he was proud of her for fighting, that he loved her and didn't blame her for what was about to happen.

Elena's world narrowed to just the two of them, the guards and the executioner mere specters at the edge of her vision. In that moment, she saw everything clearly: Aidan's kindness, his boundless curiosity, his fierce love for his family and his country. The injustice of it all was a knife twisting in her chest.

Aidan was to be thrown off a wall, falling hundreds of feet to his death. That was the way king Ulric had decided to execute his son.

The executioner, a man who had never shown the slightest trace of mercy in his lifetime, approached Aidan with a heavy heart. His eyes met Elena's, and she saw in them the same horror that reflected in hers. This wasn't just about carrying out a duty; it was about the brutal end of a young life, a life filled with potential and promise. Aiden's gaze remained unflinching, his expression a mix of anger, fear, and a fierce resolve that seemed to defy the very air around him. He knew his fate was sealed, yet he refused to show the slightest hint of weakness. His jaw was set, his eyes blazed with a fiery determination that seemed to light up the gloomy atmosphere.

The guard holding Aidan's arms tightened his grip, his eyes flicking to the side, as if seeking reassurance from his comrades. Aiden looked up at the towering figure of the executioner, who held the rope that bound his wrists. The man's face was a mask of cold, calculated indifference, his eyes as empty as the abyss that awaited the prince. Aidan took a deep breath, his chest rising and falling with the effort to remain calm. He knew that he had to be strong, not just for himself but for Elena. He couldn't let her see him break.

The wind whipped through the tower, carrying with it the distant cries of the castle's inhabitants, who had gathered below to witness the grim spectacle. Aiden felt the cold rain on his face, a cruel kiss from the world he was about to leave. His eyes searched the horizon, as if trying to drink in every last detail of the world he knew and loved. The executioner stepped closer, Aiden's heart pounded in his chest, a wild stallion desperately trying to break free from its bonds.

The rope around his wrists was pulled taut, the coarse fibers biting into his skin. He could feel the executioner's hot breath on his neck as he leaned down to whisper the final words of a prayer, a hollow comfort that seemed to echo the emptiness of the act about to be committed. Aiden's eyes remained locked with Elena's, her own a maelstrom of pain and anger. He offered her a weak smile, trying to convey the words that were trapped behind his gag.

As the executioner's hand reached for him, Aiden's thoughts raced. Memories flooded his mind, a whirlwind of moments that had shaped him into the prince he was today. He remembered the joyful laughter of his people, the stern but loving guidance of his father, the endless days of sword practice with his sister by his side, the thrill of discovery in the castle's library. And yet, none of those memories brought him peace. Instead, they fueled the fire of his anger and his determination to survive.

The executioner's hand was like a mountain pressing against his back, urging him closer to the edge. Aiden's legs trembled, not with fear, but with the sheer force of his will to resist. His eyes never left Elena's, the bond between them stronger than the chains that bound him.

With a final, brutal shove, the executioner sent Aiden hurtling through the air.

Chapter 10:

Aidan could hear his sister's pained cries as he kept falling, the ground rushing up to meet him with terrifying speed. Yet, as he plummeted towards the jungle far below, Aiden's thoughts remained surprisingly clear. He knew that he had to survive, for Elena's sake, for the sake of their father, who had been deceived by the treacherous count.

As he fell, Aiden's eyes searched the darkness for any sign of salvation. He saw the dense canopy of trees stretching out like a green sea below, and he braced himself for the impact. His body collided with a thick branch, the shock of it jolting through his bones. He felt the rough bark scrape against his skin, tearing his clothes and leaving trails of fire in their wake. The impact was enough to knock the wind out of him, but his fall didn't stop. He kept plummeting, hitting tree after tree, each collision sending a new wave of pain through his body.

The wind rushed past his ears, a deafening roar that seemed to drown out everything else. His vision blurred, and the world became a kaleidoscope of greens and browns as he tumbled through the dense foliage. His mind raced, trying to make sense of his situation, trying to find a way to survive the fall that seemed to have no end. Aiden's thoughts were a jumble of fear, anger, and a stubborn refusal to give in to the darkness that threatened to claim him.

And then, just when he thought all hope was lost, something miraculous happened. His arms, bound by the chains, shot up instinctively as he felt the rough bark of a tree branch brush against them. With a strength born of desperation, he managed to loop the chain around the thick limb, his body jolting to a sudden stop. For a moment, he hung there, suspended between life and death, the world spinning around him.

The pain was intense, his arms feeling like they were about to be torn from their sockets, but the relief was immediate. He had bought himself precious seconds, a brief reprieve from the inexorable pull of gravity. Aiden took a deep, shuddering breath, feeling the cold rain pummel his face. His vision swam, but he focused on the branch above, the lifeline that had snatched him from oblivion.

With a grunt of effort, he began to swing his body back and forth, the arc of his pendulum motion growing wider with each swing. His heart hammered in his chest, the beat echoing in his ears as he timed his movements with the rhythm of the swaying branch. Each swing brought him closer to the trunk of the tree, and with every ounce of strength he had left, he kicked his legs up, aiming for the solid embrace of the wood.

The first few attempts were clumsy, his body smacking painfully against the trunk, sending splinters flying. Yet, with the tenacity of a trapped animal, Aidan persevered. His mind was a whirlwind of thoughts and fears, but he pushed them aside, focusing solely on the task at hand. His arms burned with the strain of holding his weight, but he refused to let go.

On the fifth swing, Aiden managed to hook his leg around the branch, his body contorting in a desperate bid for purchase. For a moment, he hung there, his body a twisted knot of pain and determination. With a roar fueled by his indomitable will, he hauled himself upwards, the muscles in his arms screaming in protest. His chest heaved as he struggled to breathe, the rain stinging his eyes like a thousand needles.

The branch was wet and slippery, but Aiden's grip was like a vice, his fear lending him the strength of a dozen men. He pulled himself up, inch by agonizing inch, until he was finally able to straddle the branch, his arms and legs wrapped around it like a desperate lover clinging to a lifeline. His breaths were ragged, his heart pounding like a blacksmith's hammer against an anvil. He had cheated death, but the battle was far from over.

The chains that had bound his wrists together had become a twisted necklace of pain and salvation. He knew he had to find a way to free himself, but the thought of letting go of the branch, even for a moment, was enough to make his stomach lurch. He took a deep breath, willing his trembling body to stillness, and began to feel around the trunk of the tree with his bound hands.

The rain had made the bark slippery, and the chains bit into his skin with each movement, but he focused on the task at hand. His eyes searched the tree's surface for any small protrusions that might offer leverage. He found a knot in the wood, and with a grunt of effort, managed to work the chain around it. Slowly, painfully, he began to lower himself down the tree.

The process was torturous, his muscles screaming with each inch gained. His feet scraped against the trunk, searching for any small footholds. The chains clanked rhythmically with his movements, a macabre counterpoint to the steady patter of rain. He could feel the tree swaying slightly beneath his weight, a reminder of the precariousness of his situation.

Each time he slid the chains lower, he had to reposition his legs and adjust his grip. It was a dance of pain and balance, a dance he had never imagined performing. His hands grew numb from the cold and the constant pressure, yet he didn't dare let go. The fall was long, and the jungle floor promised no mercy.

Finally, after what felt like an eternity, Aiden's feet brushed against the soft, wet earth. He took a deep breath, his eyes closed tightly, For a moment, he hung there, suspended between the safety of the tree and the jagged embrace of the ground below. His heart hammered in his chest, a caged beast fighting for freedom.

Aiden let go, his body dropping the remaining few feet. He landed with a thud, the impact jolting through his legs and up his spine. The pain was intense, but it was a sweet agony, a reminder that he was still alive. He lay there for a moment, panting, the rain washing over him like a cold embrace.

With a grimace, he pushed himself to his knees, his muscles screaming in protest. He had to move, to get away from the castle before they realized their mistake. His eyes searched the jungle, the thick foliage a wall of shadows and whispers. The castle loomed above, a silent sentinel watching over the scene of his near-execution.

Aiden took a tentative step forward, his bound hands held out in front of him like a blind man's staff. Each movement sent waves of pain through his arms, but he gritted his teeth and persevered. The rain had turned the earth to mud, clinging to his boots and making each step feel like he was fighting through quicksand. Yet, he knew he couldn't stop. He had to find help, to clear his name and save his sister from the same fate and protect his kingdom.

The jungle was a cacophony of sounds, the rain's patter mingling with the distant calls of unseen animals. The canopy above shielded him from the worst of the downpour, but the moisture clung to him like a second skin. He stumbled on, his eyes searching the shadows for any sign of civilization, for a friendly face or a hint of the path he should take.

And then, like a beacon in the gloom, he saw a flicker of light through the trees. His heart leaped in his chest, hope flaring to life like a candle in the wind. Aiden forced his aching body to move faster, his boots squelching in the mud. As he approached, the light grew stronger, revealing a small clearing where a man was hunched over a log, his back to Aiden.

The woodcutter's saw was a tool of salvation, its teeth gleaming sharp in the firelight. With a deep breath, Aiden called out, his voice hoarse from the screams and the fall. The man whirled around, the saw held defensively. His eyes widened in surprise at the sight of the mud-splattered, chained prince standing before him.

"Please," Aiden rasped, his voice barely above a whisper, "help me."

The woodcutter, a man with a face weathered by years of labor and a beard as thick as the forest he called home, took a cautious step forward. His eyes searched Aiden's face, his gaze lingering on the bruises and the blood that marred the prince's skin. His initial shock gave way to concern, and then, recognition. "Your Highness?" he murmured, his voice filled with a mix of awe and fear.

Aiden nodded, his throat too tight to speak. He held out his bound wrists, the chains rattling like a mournful symphony. The woodcutter's gaze fell upon them, and understanding dawned in his eyes. With trembling hands, he set aside his saw and approached the prince, his eyes never leaving the chains that symbolized the injustice that had been wrought.

The man's touch was gentle, yet firm, as he took the chains in his calloused hands. He examined them closely, searching for a way to free the prince without causing further harm. His eyes narrowed in concentration, the firelight casting shadows that danced across his face. The tension in the clearing was palpable, the only sounds the rain's patter and the crackle of the fire.

With a decisive nod, the woodcutter picked up his saw, the metal glinting in the flickering light. He approached Aiden with a careful step, his movements deliberate and precise. Aiden braced himself, the anticipation of pain almost unbearable, but he knew he had no other choice. The man took hold of the chain, positioning the saw with a delicacy that belied his rough exterior.

The saw's teeth bit into the metal, sending sparks flying into the damp air. Aiden gritted his teeth, focusing on the warmth of the fire rather than the searing pain that shot up his arms. Each grating movement of the saw was a symphony of hope and agony, a testament to the unbreakable loyalty that had driven him to survive.

Finally, with a clatter, the chains fell away, the heavy links hitting the ground with a finality that seemed to echo through the jungle. Aiden brought his hands to his face, rubbing his wrists in a desperate attempt to bring back the feeling to his numb fingers. He looked up at the woodcutter, his eyes brimming with gratitude. "Thank you," he whispered, his voice hoarse from the screams that had been muffled by the gag.

The woodcutter, a man of few words, offered a solemn nod, his expression a blend of pity and admiration.

"Your Highness," he said, his voice gruff with concern, "you must get cleaned and rest. Your badly injured. "

Chapter 11:

Elena watched from the tower, her heart racing. She had seen Aiden's fall, and she knew he had to be dead. The grief was suffocating, a heavy weight pressing down on her chest, making it hard to breathe.

The woodcutter took Aiden to his humble home, nestled in the heart of the jungle. His wife, a kind woman with a gentle touch and a face lined with a lifetime of care, tended to Aiden's injuries. She washed the blood and grime from his face with warm water and wrapped his bruises with soft cloth. The warmth of the fire and the scent of cooking meat filled the air as she worked, a stark contrast to the coldness of the dungeons.

Aiden ate ravenously, the simple meal of roasted venison and tubers tasting like the most sumptuous feast he had ever enjoyed. The warmth of the food and the fire slowly spread through him, chasing away the cold that had settled deep in his bones. The woodcutter's wife, a woman named Edith, watched him with a mix of pity and determination. Despite his injuries, she could see the strength in his eyes, the unbroken spirit that had driven him to survive the fall.

As Aiden's strength began to return, the woodcutter spoke in hushed tones, sharing whispers of a rebellion growing in the outskirts of the kingdom. His words ignited a spark within the prince, a flicker of hope that grew into a flame of determination.

The woodcutter, whose name was revealed to be Thomas, listened intently as Aiden recounted his ordeal. His face grew dark with anger as he heard of his tale, and he pledged his support to the prince's cause. "My son, he was taken by Aldric's men," Thomas said, his voice thick with emotion. "If there is a chance to bring him down, I am with you, Your Highness."

The following days saw Aiden regain his strength, his body mending under Edith's care.

The siblings' bond was unbreakable, and even as Elena mourned Aiden's supposed death, she felt a glimmer of hope deep within her. It was a hope she clung to fiercely, a hope that kept her going as she plotted her escape from the castle's confines.Gloria had stayed by her side every day, comforting her, supporting her. Her mind raced with the knowledge that she had to act quickly, before her father's grip grew even tighter.

Aiden, now hidden in Thomas's hut, knew that time was of the essence. He had to let Elena know he was alive. With Thomas's help, they concocted a plan. Thomas would venture to the castle under the guise of delivering firewood, and when the opportunity arose, he would slip a message into Elena's chambers.

The next day, as dawn's early light pierced the jungle's canopy, Thomas set off with a cart laden with chopped wood. His heart heavy with the burden of the secret he carried, he approached the castle's gates. The guards, recognizing the old woodcutter, barely spared him a glance as he passed through. His eyes searched the windows for any sign of life, hoping to catch a glimpse of Elena or Gloria.

Inside the castle walls, Elena's chambers remained a prison of her own making. She had not spoken a word since Aiden's execution, her eyes hollow with grief. Gloria watched over her, a silent sentinel, her own heart torn by the loss of her friend. Yet, she knew she had to keep Elena's hope alive, to remind her that there was still a fight to be had.

The castle bustled with activity, the daily rhythms of life continuing despite the shadow of betrayal that had fallen over the royal family. Guards patrolled the corridors with renewed vigilance, their eyes searching for any sign of dissent or rebellion. The tension in the air was palpable, a storm brewing in the hearts of those who knew the truth.

Thomas approached the castle, his cart creaking under the weight of the firewood. His heart raced with the urgency of his mission, the knowledge that he held the key to setting the kingdom back on its rightful path. As he passed the guards, he offered a nod, his eyes downcast in feigned servitude. The chains that had once bound Aiden's wrists now lay hidden beneath the folds of his own cloak, a silent testament to the prince's bravery.

Finally, he reached the royal chambers, the grandeur of the castle walls a stark contrast to the modest hut he had shared with Aiden. He searched the corridors, his eyes peeled for any sign of Elena or Gloria. The castle was a labyrinth of shadows and whispers, the very stones seeming to hold their breath as he moved. His steps grew lighter, his senses sharper, as he approached the door to Elena's chamber.

With a deep breath, he rapped lightly, his heart pounding like a war drum in his chest. The door creaked open, revealing the two figures he sought. Gloria's eyes widened at the sight of him, and she stepped aside, allowing him to enter. Elena, her eyes red and swollen from days of weeping, looked up, hope and fear warring within her gaze.

Thomas stepped into the chamber, the chains still clutched in his hand. He knelt before Elena, the gravity of his words weighing on him. "Your Highness," he whispered, his voice thick with emotion, "your brother lives."

Chapter 12:

Elena's eyes widened, her breath catching in her throat. "What? How?" she demanded, her voice a mix of disbelief and desperate hope.

Thomas reached into the folds of his cloak and produced the chains that had once bound Aiden. "He used these to climb back up the tree," he explained, his voice low and urgent. "He survived, though barely. He's hurt, but he's alive, and he's safe with me."

Elena's eyes fell upon the chains, and she felt a shiver run down her spine. The metal links were tarnished with dirt and blood, a stark reminder of the horror she had witnessed. Yet, as she took them in her trembling hands, they became a symbol of hope, of Aiden's unyielding will to live. "How?" she whispered, her voice barely audible.

Gloria looked between Thomas and Elena, her own eyes wide with astonishment. She had known Aiden since they were children, had watched him grow from a mischievous boy to the prince they had all come to love. To think he had survived such a fall...it seemed impossible. Yet, as she looked into Elena's eyes, she saw the truth reflected there. The prince lived, and with him, their hope for justice.

Elena's grip on the chains tightened, her knuckles white. "Tell me everything," she said, her voice a hoarse whisper. "How did he survive? How can we be sure it's not a trick?"

Thomas met her gaze steadily, his own eyes filled with conviction. "He fell into the jungle, Your Highness," he began, his words measured and deliberate. "By some miracle, he found my home, where he is now healing. He sent me to deliver this message." He pulled a small, rolled parchment from his pocket and placed it into Elena's trembling hands. "He wants you to leave the castle tonight, under the cover of darkness, and come to me."

Elena's mind raced as she unfurled the parchment, her eyes scanning the hastily scribbled message. It was Aiden's handwriting, no doubt. The words were simple, yet filled with urgency: "Elena, I live. Meet me at Thomas's hut. We must act quickly to expose the treachery. Trust no one."

Her heart pounded in her chest as she read the words aloud to Gloria, whose eyes grew wide with astonishment. "But how can we leave?" Gloria whispered, her voice trembling with excitement. "The castle is under lock and key."

Elena took a deep, steadying breath. "We'll find a way," she said, her voice filled with the same determination that had carried Aiden through his ordeal. "We must trust Thomas."

Under the cover of night, the two young girls waited with bated breath as the castle's activities wound down. The moon had risen high, casting a silvery glow across the courtyard, turning the cobblestones to a sea of shifting shadows. The guards' footsteps grew fewer, their watchful eyes dulled by the late hour.

Elena and Gloria had prepared meticulously, their hearts beating in time with the ticking of the castle's grand clock. They had traded their royal garb for simple peasant clothes, a disguise that would allow them to blend into the shadows like whispers on the wind. The chains that once held Aiden now wrapped around Elena's waist, a grim reminder of the danger that awaited them and the bond that united them.

They waited until the castle had settled into a deep slumber, the only sound the distant toll of the midnight bell. With the chains of Aiden's survival clutched tightly in her hand, Elena slipped out of her chamber, Gloria at her side. They moved like shadows, their soft-soled shoes barely making a whisper against the cold stone floor.

The castle's corridors stretched before them like a serpent's coils, each turn and archway a potential trap. The air was thick with tension, the very walls seeming to breathe in their secrets. Yet, they moved with a purpose, their steps swift and sure, driven by the hope that burned within them.

As they approached the kitchens, they could hear the soft murmur of sleepy whispers and the clang of pans. A guard snored in a chair by the door, his helmet askew. They slipped past him, their hearts pounding a silent battle cry, and into the relative safety of the storeroom. There, they gathered supplies for their journey: food, water, and a small knife that Elena tucked into her belt.

Their escape route took them through the castle's forgotten passages, a maze of dusty corridors that had not seen the light of day in decades. The air was stale and musty, and the occasional scurry of a mouse was enough to make them jump.

But they moved with the silent grace of ghosts, each step carrying them closer to freedom and their brother's side.

After hours of careful navigation, they emerged into the cool night air, the rain having abated to a gentle mist that kissed their faces. The moon had long ago disappeared behind a veil of clouds, and the stars offered the barest of guidance. They stumbled through the jungle, their path illuminated only by the faint light that managed to filter through the dense foliage.

The journey was fraught with peril, the jungle's embrace as unforgiving as the castle's stones. Branches snagged their clothes, and roots tripped their feet. Yet, they pushed on, driven by the thought of Aiden and the injustice that had been wrought. The air grew thicker with each passing moment, the scent of damp earth and moss a constant companion as they navigated the shadowy path.

Finally, through the veil of trees, they saw the flicker of a distant light. Aiden's heart soared in his chest as he recognized the silhouettes of his sister and Gloria emerging from the darkness. The woodcutter's hut stood before them, a bastion of safety and hope amidst the treacherous jungle. The door creaked open, and Elena rushed forward, her eyes searching the shadows.

"Aiden?" she called, her voice trembling with hope and fear.

The figure that stepped into the light was indeed her brother. His clothes were tattered, his body bruised and cut from his fall, but his eyes burned with the same fiery spirit that had always been his hallmark. Elena threw herself into his arms, sobbing with relief and joy. Aiden winced at the impact but held her tightly, feeling the warmth of her embrace seep into his bones, chasing away the chill of the damp jungle night.

Thomas and Gloria looked on, their faces etched with smiles and tears. The tension of the past days seemed to melt away as the siblings hugged each other fiercely, their laughter mingling with their sobs. "I knew you weren't dead," Elena whispered into Aiden's chest, her voice muffled by his shirt.

Aiden's arms tightened around her, and he managed a weak chuckle. "You always had more faith in me than I had in myself," he murmured, his voice filled with love and relief. He stepped back, his eyes shining with unshed tears as he took in the sight of his sister. "You look like a proper jungle explorer," he teased, gesturing to her disheveled hair and mud-splattered clothes.

Elena swiped at her cheeks, her smile wobbly. "And you look like you've been wrestling a dragon," she shot back, with a wry chuckle.

Gloria stepped forward, her eyes shimmering with unshed tears. "You really had us worried, you know," she said, her voice thick with emotion. "We thought we'd lost you."

Aiden offered her a lopsided grin, his eyes never leaving Elena's. "I had to make it an unforgettable escape," he said, his voice still raw from his ordeal. "Couldn't disappoint my audience."

Chapter 13:

The woodcutter's hut was a haven of warmth and light, a stark contrast to the cold, damp jungle outside. They gathered around the fire, the flickering flames casting a warm glow on their faces. Aiden recounted his fall, his survival, and his journey to Thomas's hut, leaving no detail unspoken. His voice grew stronger with each word, the horror of his experience fading into the background as he focused on the warmth of their reunion.

Elena listened with rapt attention, her heart racing with every twist of the story. She couldn't believe that her brother had survived such a fall, that he had endured such pain and hardship. Yet, as she looked into his eyes, she saw the unyielding spirit that had always defined him. Her resolve to bring down Count Aldric grew with each word, her hatred for the man who had torn their family apart burning hotter than the fire beside her.

But their happiness was short-lived. As they sat together, sharing tales of hope and despair, a sudden unease settled over the camp. The air grew colder, the fire's warmth retreating before an unseen force. Gloria was the first to notice, her eyes widening in terror as she pointed out into the jungle. "Look," she whispered, her voice barely audible over the crackling fire. "The mist..."

A thick, blackish mist began to coil around the tree trunks, wrapping itself around the camp like a malevolent serpent. The once vibrant jungle was swallowed whole, the color leached from the world as the mist grew denser. Elena's eyes snapped to Aiden, fear etched into her features. "What is this?" she gasped.

Thomas rose to his feet, his face grim as he surveyed the spreading darkness. "This is not natural," he murmured, his eyes narrowing. "It's Aldric. He's found us." His hand reached for an axe by the fireplace, the muscles in his forearms tensing.

But before he could take a step, the mist reached out like a living entity, enveloping them in its cold, suffocating embrace. It swirled around them, thick and inky, a silent scream echoing through the night. Elena's eyes grew wide with terror, and she clutched the chains tighter. The world grew hazy, and her vision blurred at the edges. Aiden, ever the fighter, tried to stand, to defend his sister, but his legs buckled beneath him.

Gloria stumbled backward, her hand reaching out as if to ward off an invisible attacker. "No," she croaked, her voice barely audible. "Not again." But even as she spoke, her eyes rolled back in her head, and she crumpled to the ground, unconscious.

Aiden managed to hold on for a few moments longer, his eyes wide with horror as he watched the mist thicken and swirl around them. He knew what this meant—Aldric had found them, and he had brought with him the dark magic that had haunted their lives. With a roar of defiance, he tried to stand, to fight back against this new horror, but his legs gave out, and he collapsed beside his sister.

Aidan was the first to regain consciousness, his eyes slowly opening up as he scanned the unfamiliar surroundings. The warm, familiar light of Thomas's hut was replaced by the cool, early morning light of an unknown place. Elena and Gloria laid near him still unconscious as he pushed himself off the ground, his body aching from the fall and the strange, cold embrace of the mist. Panic set in as he took in the foreign sights and sounds of a place that was definitely not the jungle they had left behind.

The small, thatched-roof cottages of the outlying village of the neighboring kingdom of Lysandia greeted them, the dirt streets wet with dew and the air filled with the scent of freshly baked bread and livestock. Aiden's eyes widened in shock, taking in the unfamiliar scenery. "Where are we?" Elena mumbled, her voice thick with sleep and confusion.

Gloria stirred beside them, her eyes fluttering open to reveal the same bewilderment. They looked around frantically, trying to piece together what had happened. "How did we get here?" she whispered, her voice barely audible over the distant clucking of chickens and the low murmur of villagers beginning their day.

The friends helped each other to their feet, their heads spinning with questions and fear. The last thing Aiden remembered was the suffocating embrace of the mist, and now they found themselves in a quaint, foreign village.

The invisible barrier that stood between them and Estonia was unlike anything they had ever encountered. Each time they approached the border, an unseen force would push them back, sending them reeling to the ground. It was as if an invisible wall had been erected, one that they could not penetrate no matter how hard they tried.

Elena stumbled back, her eyes wide with shock as she rubbed her bruised forehead. "What is this sorcery?" she spat, her anger and frustration palpable. The barrier was cold, unyielding, and it seemed to pulse with a malevolent energy that made their skin crawl.

Gloria leaned heavily on Aiden, her breathing ragged. "It's got to be Aldric," she panted, her eyes flashing with determination. "He's trapped us here somehow."

Aiden's jaw tightened as he surveyed the unyielding barrier before them. The mist had been his doing, a twisted trick to separate them from the safety of the jungle and leave them vulnerable. "We need to find a way through," he said, his voice grim. "We can't let him win."

But try as they might, nothing they did could breach the invisible wall. They threw rocks, swung makeshift weapons. Each attempt was met with a repulsive force that sent them stumbling backward. It was as if the very air itself had turned against them, a tangible manifestation of their despair.

Aiden's expression grew grim as he assessed their predicament. "We need to think," he murmured, his eyes never leaving the barrier. "We can't fight this with brute strength or desperation."

Elena nodded, her own anger and fear giving way to the cold logic that had earned her the title "The Wise Scholar." They couldn't just throw themselves at the invisible wall like moths to a flame, hoping to break through. They needed a plan, a way to outsmart the cunning count who had orchestrated their exile.

They decided to blend in with the villagers, adopting the guise of orphans in search of work. The siblings and Gloria donned the simple clothes they had brought with them, tucking their royal garments away as painful reminders of their lost home. With heads bowed and eyes downcast, they made their way through the bustling streets, their hearts heavy with the weight of their secret.

Gloria took the lead, her upbringing as a commoner, a beacon in the chaos. She taught them the common tongue, the subtle gestures and behaviors that would allow them to melt into the fabric of the village unnoticed. They practiced their new personas, speaking in hushed tones and avoiding the gazes of the townsfolk.

Elena, used to the poise and grace of royalty, found it strange Yet, she knew that survival depended on their ability to adapt. Aiden, on the other hand, took to the role with surprising ease, his natural charisma and wit shining through the rough exterior he had assumed.

Their first encounter with the villagers was nerve-wracking. A kind-faced lady with a basket of freshly picked berries offered them a warm smile and a question that seemed innocent enough. "Where are your parents, children?" she asked, her eyes filled with genuine concern.

Aiden's heart skipped a beat, but he responded swiftly, his voice steady. "We're orphans, ma'am," he said, his eyes meeting hers with a mix of sadness and hope. "We've been traveling for days," added, his voice trembling just enough to sound convincing. "We're looking for work, a place to stay." Gloria said playing along, her voice filled with the same desperation.

The woman's eyes searched their faces, a flicker of doubt crossing her expression. "I am Hunith," she said finally, her tone gentle. "You look like you've seen more than your fair share of hardship." She turned and gestured to the cottage behind her. "You can stay with me and my son."

Her son, a boy named Alec, emerged from the shadows of the cottage. He was around Aiden's age, with a mop of dark hair and a smudge of dirt on his cheek. His eyes lit up at the sight of the newcomers, curiosity overshadowing any fear or suspicion. He stepped forward, his hand outstretched. "Welcome," he said with a shy smile.

The siblings and Gloria exchanged a look, their hearts warmed by the boy's kindness. They knew that trust was a rare commodity in their world, especially in times of danger and uncertainty. Hunith watched them carefully, her gaze lingering on the bruises peeking through their hastily donned disguises. "You look as though you've been through quite an ordeal," she said, her voice filled with concern. "Rest and recover here. Alec will show you around when you're feeling better."

After a simple but filling supper of stew and bread, Alec eagerly offered to show them around the village. He led them through the winding streets, chattering away about the local games and the best places to catch frogs. His enthusiasm was infectious, and despite their troubles, Elena and Aiden couldn't help but feel a spark of excitement.

Chapter 14:

The next morning, as they were helping Hunith with the chores, Alec introduced them to his friend, Jaren. He was a year older than Aiden, with a lean, muscular build and a sharp gaze that seemed to see right through their disguises. There was a hardness to him that spoke of a life of struggle, a stark contrast to the jovial atmosphere of the village. "My dad was a soldier," Jaren said, his voice laced with bitterness as they worked side by side in the fields. "He died fighting for a king who cared more about his gold than the lives of his men."

The words hit Aiden like a slap in the face, but he knew better than to argue. The pain in Jaren's eyes was too raw, too real. Instead, he focused on the task at hand, planting seeds with a determination that matched his newfound resolve to take down Count Aldric. Elena and Gloria worked alongside them, their movements silent and efficient as they listened to the boy's story.

"But one of the things we do for fun around here," Alec said, his eyes twinkling with mischief. "is to play tricks on old man Simon."

Aiden's ears perked up at the mention of the grumpy old noble. "What do you mean?"

Alec grinned, the corners of his eyes crinkling. "He's a bit of a grump, but that just adds to the fun," he whispered, leaning in conspiratorially.

Aiden's mind raced with ideas, his mischievous spirit rekindling. "I've got the perfect trick," he said, his eyes gleaming. "Back at my village, I was legendary for my pranks."

Gloria froze, her hands hovering over a basket of freshly picked berries. "Aiden," she warned, her eyes narrowed.

Elena rolled her eyes, recognizing the mischievous glint in her brother's gaze. "What now?" she sighed, already knowing that she would likely have to clean up whatever mess he was about to make.

But Aiden was already making his move as he and Alec ran to old man Simon's house, their laughter echoing through the quiet morning air. Gloria and Elena exchanged a knowing look before following, unable to completely suppress their curiosity. They approached the small, well-kept cottage with caution, their steps quickening as they heard the sound of something being dragged across the wooden porch.

As they turned the corner, they saw Aiden and Alec had already set the stage for their prank. The girl, a pretty young thing with a penchant for frills and lace, was standing there, her cheeks flushed with excitement. Alec whispered something in her ear, and she giggled, nodding eagerly. Aiden grinned at the sight, his eyes alight with the thrill of the prank.

The granddaughter of Old Man Simon, Lila was known around the village for her love of fashion and her tendency to get lost in her own world. She had been recruited as the unsuspecting accomplice in their plot. With her help, they had constructed a makeshift contraption that looked suspiciously like a royal carriage, made from wooden planks and painted with berry juice. It was a masterpiece of imagination and resourcefulness that could only come from the minds of two young boys looking for a laugh.

As Lila took her place in the "carriage," her grandpa's favorite chair atop the planks, they painted an elaborate story for her to tell Old Man Simon. She was to claim that a mysterious prince had arrived in the night and had bestowed upon her a magical ride through the village. Her performance had to be convincing enough to distract him from the chaos they were about to cause.

Aiden and Alec crouched behind a nearby bush, their hearts racing as they waited for the perfect moment to spring their trap. The tension grew as they heard the old man's shuffling footsteps approaching his cottage. Lila persuaded her grandfather to take a seat on the contraption as she started to tell him her dramatic tale. The boys counted to three and gave the contraption a mighty shove. It careened down the cobblestone street, the chair teetering precariously, Their laughter ringing out like music.

Lila played her part to perfection, her eyes wide with wonder as she described the enchanted carriage that had brought her back from her royal escapades. Old man Simon, his curiosity piqued, his expression a mix of confusion and irritation.

Meanwhile, hidden from view, Aiden and Alec couldn't contain their snickers as they watched the scene unfold. The "carriage" gathered speed, the chair wobbling dangerously as it bumped over the uneven cobblestones. The villagers, drawn by the commotion, peered out of their windows and doors, their expressions a blend of amusement and bewilderment.

The prank reached its climax as the chair collided with a strategically placed pile of mud, sending old man simons tumbling into the gooey mess. Old man Simon's eyes grew as wide as dinner plates as he took in the sight, his pristine chair, and the trail of berry stains leading back to the bushes. The boys had hoped for surprise and a good laugh, but what they got was an explosion of fury from the usually stoic nobleman.

With a roar that seemed to shake the very earth beneath them, Old Man Simon lurched to his feet, fists clenched and eyes blazing. "You little devils!" he bellowed, his voice carrying over the now-silent street. "I'll have your hides for this!"

Aiden and Alec didn't need a second invitation. They bolted from their hiding place, their laughter pealing through the early morning air as they sprinted away from the irate nobleman. The chase was on, the boys' legs pumping with the excitement of the moment. Aiden could feel the adrenaline coursing through his veins, pushing him to run faster, to stay one step ahead of the wrath that pursued them.

Their boots slapped against the dirt streets, sending up little puffs of dust that danced in the early light. Old Man Simon huffed and puffed in pursuit, his fury seemingly giving him a surprising burst of speed. The villagers watched with a mix of horror and amusement, some ducking back into their homes while others cheered the boys on. The air was thick with the scent of the mud that now coated Old Man Simon's clothes, a stark reminder of the chaos they had wrought.

Elena and Gloria, who had been watching the prank unfold from a safe distance, couldn't help but laugh at the sight of the grumpy nobleman covered in muck. But as the chase grew more intense, they bolted after the boys, their own laughter mingling with the chaos. The villagers parted before them, some shouting warnings, others cheering the spectacle.

Chapter 15:

Days turned into weeks, and the siblings and Gloria had blended into the village quite nicely. They worked hard alongside Hunith and Alec, helping with the chores and learning the rhythms of village life. Elena's natural grace made her adept at weaving and cooking, while Aiden found an unexpected talent for mending fences and tending to the livestock. Gloria, ever the quick learner, proved to be a skilled herbalist, much to Hunith's delight.

Yet, the shadow of their true identities and the unyielding barrier that separated them from their homeland loomed over their heads. They spoke in hushed whispers about their plight, sharing theories and half-formed plans late into the night. The villagers had come to accept them as their own, sharing stories of their own struggles and hardships. It was a simple existence, but it was filled with a warmth and camaraderie that the siblings hadn't known since their mother's passing.

However Aiden, Elena and Gloria weren't the only ones with a secret. Alec and his mother had their own secret one they never dared speak of. Alec had been born with powerful magic, capable of moving objects with his thoughts alone among other thing. His mother, Hunith, had recognized the signs early, the way a spoon would twirl in mid-air when he was upset or a toy would glide to his outstretched hand when he was happy.

But she had also seen the fear in people's eyes when they caught a glimpse of his abilities. The whispers of witchcraft and dark magic had followed them like a shadow. To protect her son, Hunith had forbidden Alec from using his powers. She had hoped that by hiding his gift, he would be safe from the suspicion and violence that often accompanied those who were different.

Aiden and Alec had grown very close in the short time they had been together. They were like two sides of the same coin, unalike in their circumstances but bound by their shared mischief and the burden of secrets they each carried. Aiden's charm and bravado balanced Alec's quiet strength and burgeoning power, and Alec's steadfastness grounded Aiden's impulsive spirit.

One chilly evening, as they returned from the fields, Aiden spotted something peculiar in the corner of the cottage. Alec was hunched over the hearth, his eyes closed and his small hands cupped around a flickering flame. From the heart of the fire, a delicate, iridescent dragon took shape, its wings fluttering gracefully as it danced upon the heat. The prince's eyes widened in amazement. He had never seen such a display of magic. His father had drilled into Aiden's head that all magic was evil but he didn't truly believe it and now he saw Alec using magic and it was so beautiful.

For a moment, Aiden was transfixed by the sight, his heart swelling with a mix of awe and wonder. The dragon twisted and turned, a living sculpture of fire that seemed to respond to Alec's every thought. Then, as if sensing his presence, Alec's eyes snapped open, and the dragon dissipated into a puff of sparks. The room grew quiet, and Alec looked up at him, his expression a mix of shock and fear.

"I'm sorry," Aiden said quickly, his voice barely above a whisper. "I didn't mean to spy."

Alec looked at him, his eyes wide with shock. "It's okay," he said after a moment, his voice shaking. "But you must promise never to tell anyone."

Aiden nodded solemnly, his gaze still lingering on the spot where the dragon had been. He had grown up with the same fears and prejudices that most of Estonia held towards magic, but what he had just witnessed was nothing like the dark, twisted power that his father, King Ulric, had warned him about. This was something pure, something that brought joy and wonder. It was a stark contrast to the cold, calculating treachery of Count Aldric, whose magic had brought them to this unfamiliar village.

For days, the sight of the fiery dragon remained etched in Aiden's mind. He found himself watching Alec more closely, looking for signs of the power that lay dormant beneath the boy's shy exterior. Alec, on the other hand, grew more cautious, aware that he had let his guard down. Their friendship grew tentative as a silent understanding passed between them.

One evening, as they sat around the crackling fireplace, Aiden decided it was time to share his own secret. He took a deep breath and met Alec's eyes. "There's something I need to tell you," he began, his voice low and serious. "You're not the only one here with a secret."

Alec's eyes widened, his curiosity piqued. Gloria and Elena looked up from their sewing, sensing the shift in the room's energy. "What do you mean?" Alec asked, his voice tentative.

Aiden took another deep breath, his heart hammering in his chest. "We're not just orphans looking for work," he confessed. "We're actually... we're from the Royal family of Estonia. I'm Prince Aiden, and this is my sister, Elena, and our friend, Gloria."

The room grew still as the weight of Aiden's words settled over them. Alec's eyes grew as big as saucers, his mouth agape with shock. Hunith looked up from her knitting, her needles frozen in midair. "You're jesting," she said, her voice barely audible.

But Aiden's expression remained serious. He reached into his tunic and pulled out the royal crest, a lion rampant on a field of purple, that he had kept hidden since their arrival. The crest glinted in the firelight, the gold threads still vibrant despite the wear and tear of their journey. "We were falsely accused of treason by Count Aldric," he said, his voice steady. "He used dark magic to frame us and take over our kingdom."

Alec stared at the crest in awe, his fear replaced by a flicker of hope. If Aiden, a prince, could trust him with such a profound revelation, perhaps he could trust Aiden with his own secret. He took a deep breath and spoke, his words tumbling out in a rush. "I have magic," he confessed, his eyes searching Aiden's for any sign of rejection or horror. "But it's not like the dark magic Aldric uses. It's... it's just a part of me."

The room remained still as Aiden took in Alec's words. His own experiences with magic had been limited to the lessons he'd learned from his father, who had painted it as an abomination that brought only destruction and chaos. But the warmth in Alec's eyes and the gentle way he'd created the fiery dragon spoke of a different kind of power, one born of wonder and light. "I know," Aiden said, his voice gentle. "I saw what you did with the flame that day."

Alec's cheeks flushed with color, and he looked down at his hands as if they might betray him. "You didn't tell anyone?" he whispered, his voice filled with relief.

Aiden reached over and placed a reassuring hand on Alec's shoulder. "Of course not," he said firmly. "And I won't. But you need to understand, Alec, that what you have is a gift, not a curse."

Alec looked up at Aiden, his eyes searching the prince's face for any trace of deceit. He saw none, only a sincere belief that seemed to light the prince's eyes from within. "How can you be sure?" Alec asked, his voice trembling.

Aiden leaned in closer, his eyes earnest. "Because what I saw in you, that spark of creation and joy, that's not the work of darkness," he said firmly. "Dark magic is about control and fear. What you have, it brings warmth and wonder. It's a gift that could help us all."

Elena set aside her sewing and moved to join the two boys by the fire, her eyes soft with understanding. "Aiden's right," she said, placing a comforting hand on Alec's other shoulder. "And we're here for you, no matter what." Gloria nodded in agreement, her expression a mix of admiration and affection.

Alec looked at them all, his eyes shining. He had never felt so accepted, so understood. The fear that had been a constant companion for as long as he could remember began to ebb away, replaced by a warmth that spread through his chest like the embrace of a long-lost friend.

Elena chuckled, her laughter light and infectious. "Imagine if we could pull off a prank with your magic, Alec," she said, nudging him playfully. "The look on Old Man Simon's face when you conjure a flock of geese to chase him down the street."

Gloria couldn't help but join in the merriment, her laughter tinkling like the bells on the village's old church tower. "Or what if we painted the town hall with invisible paint that only appears when it rains?" she suggested, her eyes alight with mischief.

Aiden's idea was more chaotic "What if we made it rain jellyfish in the village square?"

Elena's eyes sparkled with amusement, and she playfully smacked her brother's arm. "Now that would be a sight," she said, her voice filled with warmth. "But maybe we should save the jellyfish for a special occasion."

Alec couldn't help but chuckle at the absurdity of their suggestions, feeling a weight lifted from his shoulders. He had never felt this kind of camaraderie before, not even with the other children in the village. These friends, these royals in disguise, accepted him for who he was, magic and all.

Chapter 16:

Hunith watched from the shadows, her heart swelling with pride. Her son had always been a loner, but here he was, sharing his deepest secret with these newfound friends. She had feared that his gift would always set him apart, but maybe, just maybe, it could be the thing that brought him closer to others.

Elena leaned over to whisper in Alec's ear, her eyes sparkling with mischief. "We'll have to think of something extra special for Old Man Simon next time," she said, and the four of them erupted into laughter once more. Hunith couldn't help but smile at the sound, feeling a warmth spread through her chest that had been absent for too long.

Gloria playfully ruffled Alec's hair, her eyes shining with sisterly affection. "Don't worry, we've got your back," she said, her voice filled with the confidence that had seen them through so much already. Hunith watched as the four of them huddled together, their heads bent in conspiracy, and she felt a swell of pride that her son had found such loyal companions in these strange times.

Their laughter filled the cozy cottage, the sound echoing off the wooden beams and mingling with the crackle of the fire. It was a sound that Hunith had not heard in years, not since before the dark whispers had started about Alec's abilities. Her heart felt lighter as she listened to them, their friendship a balm to her worried soul.

Elena scooted closer to Alec, her arm slipping around his shoulders in a gentle embrace. "We're all in this together," she said, her voice warm with reassurance. "We'll figure out how to get back to Estonia, and we'll make sure that Count Aldric gets what's coming to him."

Aiden's smile was gentle as he nodded in agreement. "And when we do, you'll be able to show everyone the true power of your magic," he added, his eyes gleaming with excitement at the prospect of an epic prank. "Just imagine the look on his face when we ride in with a dragon at our side!"

Elena couldn't help but giggle at the thought, her earlier worries momentarily forgotten. She moved closer to Alec, wrapping her arm around his shoulders. "We're your family now," she whispered, her voice warm with sincerity. "And we won't let anyone hurt you."

Hunith watched the exchange, her heart swelling with a pride she had never felt before. Her son, her little Alec, had finally found friends who saw him not for his magic, but for the kind, gentle soul he truly was. She had always feared that his gift would isolate him, but here he was, sharing jokes and laughter with a prince and a princess. It was a moment she had never dared to dream of, and it brought tears of joy to her eyes.

The friendship between Alec, Aiden, Elena, and Gloria grew stronger with each passing day. They worked alongside the villagers, sharing in their struggles and their triumphs. The pranks continued, though now they were more elaborate, often involving Alec's magic. The villagers grew to love the mysterious orphans, and the four of them had become a beloved part of the community's fabric.

But the laughter and camaraderie didn't distract them from their ultimate goal. They spent their evenings huddled around the fireplace, strategizing and training. Elena and Gloria taught Alec and Aiden the subtleties of courtly politics, while Aiden and Alec worked tirelessly to hone Alec's magical abilities. It was a strange juxtaposition of worlds—royalty and peasantry, light and shadow—but it was a bond that grew stronger with each spell cast and each secret shared.

Under the watchful eye of his new friends, Alec's powers grew more potent and precise. His flaming dragon grew more intricate, and he could now control the fire without setting the room ablaze. Elena, who had a knack for strategy, helped him to channel his magic into more useful forms, like creating illusions and enhancing their physical prowess. Aiden's curiosity about magic was insatiable, and he eagerly absorbed every lesson Alec offered, seeing in it a way to protect his sister and restore their kingdom.

The siblings, meanwhile, taught Alec the ways of the court—how to speak and act like royalty, so that when they returned to Estonia, he could stand beside them as an equal. They practiced dueling with sticks in the fields, the siblings' royal tutelage turning him into a formidable fighter. Gloria, ever the sneak, showed him how to navigate the shadows unseen, a skill she had honed in the castle's hidden passageways.

Elena's eyes gleamed with excitement as she watched Alec's magic grow more powerful by the day. She saw the potential in his gift, not just for mischief, but for justice. "Imagine," she said, her voice low and filled with determination, "if we could use your magic to expose Aldric's lies, to show the people of Estonia the truth of what he's done."

Aiden nodded, his thoughts racing with the possibilities. "We could infiltrate his circle, gather evidence," he mused. "Or better yet, disguise ourselves as entertainers and pull a trick so grand, it'll leave him red-faced and powerless."

Elena leaned back, her gaze thoughtful. "We'll need to be clever," she said, tapping her chin with a slender finger. "We can't just charge in blindly. We have to be strategic."

Aiden nodded in agreement, his eyes sparkling with mischief. "We'll need a plan," he said, his voice filled with the excitement of an impending adventure. "Something that will not only expose Aldric but also show the people of Estonia that magic isn't something to be feared."

The days grew shorter, and the nights grew colder as winter approached. Despite the harsh weather, the group's training sessions grew longer and more intense. Alec's control over his powers grew steadily, and his ability to manipulate fire was now nothing short of mesmerizing, he could form illusions with ease. Hunith would often bring them food and drink during these sessions, and the sight of a young boy conjuring a fiery spectacle in their makeshift arena would make her chuckle.

The laughter that filled the cottage grew more heartfelt and frequent. Hunith found that the simple act of watching Alec's magic, and the way it brought joy to her new friends, was a balm for her own fears. The jovial atmosphere was a stark contrast to the tension that had once filled the space, a testament to the healing power of friendship and acceptance.

The day finally came when the siblings and Gloria looked at Alec and knew it was time. The prince's eyes were determined, his sister's gaze was sharp with strategy, and Gloria's posture was poised and ready for action. They had practiced and prepared, turning Alec's innate abilities into a formidable weapon against the darkness that had claimed their home.

Aiden spoke up, his voice firm and resolute. "We're ready," he said, looking at Elena and Gloria. "We have Alec's magic, and we have each other. We'll return to Estonia and show the people the truth about Aldric."

Elena nodded, her eyes gleaming with a fiery resolve that mirrored the embers in the hearth. "We'll need to be careful," she warned. "But we can't wait any longer. Our people need us."

With that, they made their final preparations, donning their warmest cloaks and packing their meager belongings. Hunith watched them with a mix of pride and anxiety, her hands clenching into fists at her sides. She had grown to love these three, who had brought so much light into her and Alec's lives.

The journey to the barrier was quiet, their laughter and jokes replaced by solemn determination. The closer they got, the more the air seemed to thicken with anticipation. The barrier loomed ahead, a shimmering veil that separated them from their homeland, a stark reminder of the treachery that awaited them.

Aiden tightened his grip on his sword, the weight of his responsibility heavy on his shoulders. He had to be the shield that protected his sister and their newfound friend. Alec stood beside him, his eyes closed, hands outstretched as he began to weave a spell that would challenge the very fabric of the barrier. The air grew hot, and the scent of scorched earth filled the space around them as he summoned forth a fiery tornado, a symbol of his growing power.

Elena and Gloria took positions behind them, their bows drawn with arrows tipped with Elena's enchanted crystals. The shimmering projectiles were a last resort, a desperate attempt to pierce the veil that Count Aldric had cast over their homeland. They watched as Alec's magic grew, the tornado swirling into a maelstrom of heat and light that danced and crackled with an energy none of them had ever felt before.

Aiden stepped forward, sword in hand, and as Alec released the fiery storm towards the barrier, he sliced through the air with a warrior's cry. The blade met the flames with a clash that echoed through the barrier, sending sparks flying in every direction. The barrier shuddered, the colors within it swirling like a storm-tossed sea. Gloria and Elena let their arrows fly, each one a beacon of hope that pierced the air with a high-pitched whistle.

The arrows hit the barrier with a resounding boom, each one exploding into a burst of light that illuminated the surrounding landscape. The ground trembled beneath their feet, and the air was filled with the scent of ozone. The barrier began to crack, the fissures spreading like spider webs across a pane of glass. Alec's eyes grew wide with the power surging through him, his body glowing with the intensity of his magic.

Aiden watched, his heart racing, as the barrier's shimmer grew more erratic. The flaming maelstrom Alec had conjured grew larger, a fiery beacon of hope against the backdrop of the darkened sky. With a roar, Aiden charged forward, sword raised high, and as he did, Elena and Gloria loosed their final volley of arrows. They struck the weakened barrier with the precision of seasoned warriors, shattering it into a million shards that rained down like fiery embers.

The barrier buckled under the combined might of their determination, the cracks widening into a yawning gap. The four friends stared at the opening, their breaths coming in ragged gasps. This was it, their one chance to reclaim what was rightfully theirs. Aiden took a step forward, sword still ablaze with Alec's magic.

"Now," he shouted over the roar of the dying barrier, "we go home!"

Chapter 17:

Aiden stepped through the gap first, the fiery aura of Alec's magic still surrounding him. The air on the other side was colder. Elena and Gloria followed closely, their eyes scanning the horizon for any signs of trouble. Alec brought up the rear, his breathing labored from his exertion, but a smile of triumph lighting up his face.

The moment they were all through, Aiden turned to face the barrier, his sword still alight. He knew that this wasn't the end of the battle, just the beginning. "We'll need to keep moving," he said, his voice steady "Aldric will know we've broken through."

They set off into the night, the only sound their footsteps and the distant howl of the wind. The once familiar land of Estonia felt foreign and hostile. The vibrant fields and forests of their youth had withered under Aldric's reign, the people they encountered looked haggard and beaten, their eyes devoid of the warmth and hope that had once been so prevalent in their kingdom. Aiden's heart clenched as he took in the stark transformation. The laughter of playing children had been replaced by the whispers of fear, the greenery of the countryside by the oppressive shadow of the castle that loomed ahead.

As they approached the outskirts of the first village, word of their arrival spread like wildfire. The sight of Aiden, the prince they had believed dead, walking with a fiery aura and a band of unlikely companions, brought shock and disbelief. Then, as the recognition set in, it turned into hope. Whispers grew into shouts, and soon the villagers were running towards them, faces alight with joy and astonishment. They had been told that magic was evil, that the very air they breathed was tainted by the prince's treachery, but here he was, standing tall and strong, surrounded by friends who had the power to challenge the fabric of the dark spell that had been woven over their lands.

Elena felt a swell of pride in her chest as the people called out to her, their voices a symphony of hope and defiance. She had always known her brother's spirit was unbreakable, and now she saw the same spark in the eyes of these villagers. They had suffered under Aldric's tyranny for too long, but now they had a beacon of light to follow. The cheers grew louder as they entered the village square, where the once vibrant market stalls now stood empty and decayed.

Gloria's eyes searched the faces in the crowd, looking for any sign of deception or hidden malice. But all she saw was genuine warmth and relief. These were her people, the ones her friends had sworn to serve and protect, and she would not let them down. She tightened her grip on her bow, ready to stand alongside Aiden and Elena as they faced whatever dangers lay ahead.

The siblings and their companions moved through the throngs of villagers, the sea of faces parting before them like a wave. Aiden's laughter grew louder, his heart swelling with every shout of "the prince cheated death!" and "our saviors have arrived!" The joy in the air was palpable, a stark contrast to the fear that had suffocated the land.

Elena's eyes searched the crowd, finding the faces of those who had been there when she and Aiden had been cast out, now alight with hope. She raised a hand in a regal wave, her smile warm and genuine. "We are here for you," she called out, her voice carrying over the din. "We will not rest until Estonia is free from Aldric's shadow!"

Aiden's laughter grew louder, his heart swelling with each cheer that met his ears. He looked back at Alec, whose wide eyes reflected the wonder of it all. "They're not just my people," he said, his voice filled with pride. "They're yours too." He clapped Alec on the back, his grip firm and reassuring. "You're part of this now, more than you know."

The villagers grew bolder, reaching out to touch the cloaks of the royals, as if to make sure they weren't a mirage. Alec looked at his own hands, the fire dancing across his fingertips, and then at Aiden's sword, which still burned with a fiery aura. "I never thought... I could be a hero," he murmured, his voice filled with awe.

Aiden grinned back at him, the light of the flaming blade casting a warm glow on his face. "You've always been one, Alec," he said, his voice firm with belief. "You just needed to find the right people to fight alongside."

The crowd grew thicker as they moved through the village, people spilling out of their homes to catch a glimpse of the returned prince and princess. Children ran alongside them, their laughter mingling with the shouts of adults. Alec felt a warmth spread through him, a feeling he hadn't known since he was a small child, before his powers had manifested and made him an outcast.

He watched as Aiden and Elena interacted with the villagers, their faces alight with joy and hope. The prince and princess didn't treat the common folk as subjects to be feared or controlled, but as equals to be loved and protected. It was vastly different to the tales he had heard of the distant kings and queens who ruled from their ivory towers, disconnected from the lives of the people they governed.

Elena bent down to listen to a young girl's whispered words, her eyes kind and her smile genuine. Aiden hoisted a child onto his shoulders, his laughter ringing out as the crowd chuckled. Alec felt his own heart swell with a warmth he had never known. He had always felt like an outcast in Lysandia, feared for his magic, but here, with these people, he was accepted.

He watched as the siblings moved through the crowd, their every gesture filled with grace and compassion. The villagers reached out to touch them, as if the mere brush of their fingers could absorb some of the hope they brought with them. The prince and princess didn't shy away from the contact; instead, they embraced it, their eyes lighting up with every greeting, every tale of woe they heard.

Alec couldn't believe it—he had never seen a royal so loved by their people. The only interactions he had ever witnessed were those of fear and suspicion, but here, in the heart of this long-suffering land, Aiden and Elena were met with open arms and tearful smiles. It was a stark reminder of the difference between the true rulers and the usurper who had taken their place.

As they approached the castle gates, the crowd grew thicker, their voices a cacophony of hope and desperation. Alec's heart raced as he looked at Aiden, who seemed to grow taller with every step, his fiery aura a beacon that promised salvation. The prince's eyes never left the castle, his jaw set in a determined line that brooked no doubt—he would not rest until the dark count was brought to justice.

The villagers parted before them like a sea before Moses, their faces a mix of awe and hope. They whispered prayers and well-wishes as the four friends moved through the throng. Alec felt a strange sense of belonging, as if he had been born to this moment, to stand alongside these two siblings and help them reclaim their birthright.

Chapter 18:

The castle loomed in the distance, its dark stones stark against the night sky. Aiden's eyes never left it, his steps sure and unwavering. He had been born to be king, and now he was ready to fight for it. The crowd grew denser as they approached the gates, their voices a crescendo of determination that seemed to bolster Aiden's own resolve.

The villagers had come to know Aiden and Elena as their own, and they were not about to let them face the darkness of the castle alone. They had suffered under Aldric's rule for too long, and now, with the prince and princess returned, they had a glimmer of hope. They had seen the fire in Aiden's eyes and the steel in Elena's, and they knew that together, they could reclaim their land.

As the four friends approached the castle gates, the clatter of horse hooves grew louder, and a contingent of knights, led by Sir Marcus, appeared through the mist. The children's hearts raced as they watched the men in armor draw closer, unsure if they were friend or foe. But as they emerged from the shadows, it was clear—their banners bore the emblem of the true Estonian throne, a golden lion on a field of purple.

The knights dismounted, their faces a mix of shock and relief at the sight of the siblings they had believed dead. They embraced Aiden and Elena, whispering words of allegiance and regret for their earlier doubts. Sir Marcus, his eyes wet with emotion, fell to one knee before them. "Your Highnesses," he said, his voice trembling, "we had lost all hope. The king—he has been enchanted. Count Aldric has been pulling the strings all along."

The revelation hung in the air like a heavy shroud. Aiden's jaw clenched, his grip on the fiery sword tightening. "Our father," he said, his voice thick with emotion. "We must save him. He is not to blame for what has happened here."

Elena's eyes searched the horizon, her mind racing. "We will," she assured him. "But first, we must deal with the monster that has wrought this havoc."

Their conversation was cut short by the sudden appearance of a figure atop the castle's highest tower. The moonlight glinted off his armor, and the air grew colder as a malevolent laugh echoed through the night. Count Aldric had emerged, and with him, an army of skeletons, their bones clicking and clacking in an unholy symphony of darkness.

The skeletons swarmed from the castle's depths like a plague of the undead, their eyes burning with an unnatural light that sent shivers down the spines of the gathered villagers. Alec felt his stomach twist in fear, but he forced himself to stand tall beside Aiden and Elena, who faced the onslaught with unwavering determination.

"On me!" Aiden roared, his fiery blade held high. The knights of Estonia rallied around him, their own swords and spears glinting in the moonlight. Alec watched as Aiden's fiery aura grew, enveloping the knights in a fierce warmth that seemed to bolster their spirits. His heart swelled with pride as he realized the true depth of Aiden's bravery.

"You and Gloria," Aiden said, turning to Elena, "find the artifact. It's the source of his power. Without it, he can't control the undead." His eyes searched hers, the unspoken understanding passing between them. This was a battle they had trained for, a battle they had been born to fight.

Elena nodded, her grip tight on her bow. "We won't let you down," she assured him, before sprinting towards the castle with Gloria at her side. The two girls moved with the grace of seasoned warriors, their feet silent on the cold, hard ground. They knew the layout of the castle like the back of their hands, and they had a plan.

Aiden turned to Alec, his eyes filled with a fierce determination. "Stay with the knights, Alec," he instructed. "Your magic will be our greatest weapon against these creatures... As for me, I have an old score to settle with count Dracula over there" Alec nodded, his own fear momentarily forgotten in the face of Aiden's courage.

The knights, fueled by the return of their prince, let out a battle cry that echoed through the night, and charged towards the advancing skeletal horde. The sound of steel on bone filled the air as the knights clashed with the undead soldiers. Aiden's sword sliced through the darkness, leaving a trail of fire in its wake. Each blow was met with the shattering of bones and the wailing of unnatural spirits.

Meanwhile, Elena and Gloria darted into the castle, their eyes scanning the corridors for any sign of the artifact. They knew it was hidden somewhere within the labyrinthine fortress, a relic of power that Aldric had used to control the dead. They moved swiftly and silently, their every step calculated. They had to be careful; the castle was a maze of secrets and dangers, and they didn't know what awaited them in the shadows.

The castle walls whispered with the echoes of their footsteps, the cold stones seemingly alive with malicious intent. Elena's heart raced as she thought of her brother and Alec outside, facing the horde of undead. She had to find the artifact, had to save them all. Gloria, ever the loyal servant, stayed close, her eyes sharp and ready for any threat that might cross their path.

They climbed the narrow staircase, each step a silent promise to restore peace to their kingdom. The air grew colder, heavier with each floor they ascended, the stench of decay and dark magic thickening with each breath they took. Elena's hand brushed against the wall, and she felt a shiver run down her spine, a reminder of the malevolent force that resided within these hallowed halls.

"Remember," she whispered to Gloria, her voice barely audible over the distant clang of swords and shrieks of the undead, "the artifact must be in the highest chamber, where Father's throne used to be."

Outside Alec summoned a tornado that swept the undead soldiers clearing a path for Aiden who chased after the count.

Aiden's eyes never left Count Aldric's retreating figure as he sprinted up the castle steps, two at a time. The laughter had faded from the count's lips, replaced by a snarl of rage as he realized his enemies had breached the defenses. The air grew colder as the count's dark magic thickened, coating the walls and floor with a slick, shadowy substance.

HEIR OF THE FALLEN CROWN

In the courtyard below, Alec and the knights of Estonia faced the tide of skeletal warriors. The young warlock's fire magic danced in the night, a fiery ballet that sent the undead reeling. Each time his flames kissed the bones, they shattered into dust, freeing the trapped souls with a mournful wail. The knights fought valiantly beside him, their swords flashing in the erratic light, their shields a steadfast wall against the relentless tide of darkness.

Aiden pursued Count Aldric through the castle's winding corridors, the clang of steel and the stench of necromancy a grim soundtrack to their cat-and-mouse game. The count's cackles grew fainter with each passing moment, his footsteps echoing like the taunts of a ghost. The castle's very stones seemed to pulse with malice, the air thick with the weight of his dark power. Yet Aiden did not falter. With each stride, he drew closer to the man who had stolen his family's throne.

In the courtyard, Alec's fiery dance grew more frenetic as the skeletal warriors closed in. The knights of Estonia fought like demigods, their swords and shields a whirlwind of steel and valor. The villagers, who had once feared and shunned magic, watched in awe as he bent the very elements to his will, turning the tide of battle with every fiery gust. The undead faltered before the combined might of Alec's magic and the knights' steel, their bones shattering and spirits dispersed in a burst of light with each contact.

Yet, even as they pushed back the tide, the castle's darkened windows began to glow with an eerie light. Count Aldric had not been idle during their approach. The very stones of the fortress seemed to tremble in anticipation of the final confrontation. Aiden's eyes narrowed, his gaze fixed on the retreating figure of the count. He knew that Alec and the knights could hold the line, and that his sister and Gloria were searching for the artifact that would sever the count's connection to his unholy army.

The corridors grew narrower, the shadows deeper, until Aiden found himself in a chamber that had once been a place of great beauty—his family's throne room. Now, it was a twisted parody of its former self, the walls adorned with the grinning skulls of animals, the floor a mosaic of bones of those dared defy the count. In the center of the room stood the count, his hands aloft, dark energy coalescing around him as he chanted an incantation that sent a shiver of revulsion down Aiden's spine.

The prince charged, his sword ablaze with the fire of his determination. The count turned, his eyes glowing with malevolent power, and met Aiden's charge with a bolt of shadow that cracked through the air. The room filled with the stench of brimstone and the sizzle of magic meeting metal. Aiden's blade, imbued with Alec's fire, cleaved through the darkness, leaving a trail of light in its wake.

The battle raged on, a dance of fire and shadow. Aiden's strikes were swift and precise, each one aimed at the heart of the count's power. Aldric countered with a flurry of dark spells, his eyes never leaving Aiden's as he retreated further into the bowels of the castle. The ground trembled with each clash of wills, the very fabric of the chamber seeming to tear apart. The air was alive with the electricity of their power, a silent testament to the fury that had been unleashed.

Outside, Alec's fiery tornado grew in intensity, a beacon of hope in the face of the relentless onslaught of skeletal soldiers.

His eyes, filled with a fierce determination, never left the battle before him as he directed the inferno, guiding it to strike at the heart of the enemy ranks. The knights of Estonia, their spirits bolstered by the prince's valor, fought with renewed vigor. Each time a skeleton fell, the light grew stronger, the shadow of the castle's grip over the land receding slightly.

Inside, Elena and Gloria reached the chamber where the artifact was rumored to be hidden. The room was a cacophony of arcane symbols and dark incantations, the very air thick with the stench of corrupted magic. Elena's eyes searched the room, her hand tight around an arrow, ready to strike if needed.

"The artifact," she murmured, spotting a glowing crystal orb nestled on a pedestal shrouded in shadows. "It's here."

Gloria nodded, her eyes darting around the room. "But we're not alone."

Chapter 19:

A chilling cackle filled the air as a group of shadowy figures emerged from the dark corners, their forms twisted and inhuman. "Welcome, my dear" The voice boomed, echoed through the chamber. "How kind of you to join me in my sanctum."

Elena's eyes narrowed, her grip tightening on her bow. "You will not lay a hand on the artifact," she declared. "We have come to end this nightmare."

The shadowy figures, once hidden in the corner, took the form of twisted, malformed guards. "And who might you be," the deep, disembodied voice boomed, "to challenge the power of Count Aldric?"

Elena's voice was steady. "I am Elena, The princess of Estonia. And you shall not stand in our way."

One of the twisted guards lunged forward, its shadowy sword slicing through the air. Gloria stepped in front of her, her own blade flashing in the dim light. The clang of steel on steel rang through the chamber as she met the creature's attack with a fierce warrior's cry.

"We fight for our kingdom!" Elena shouted, loosing an arrow at the nearest guard. It shimmered with a silver light, piercing the darkness and embedding itself in the creature's chest. The shadowy figure dissipated into nothingness, the crystal on the pedestal pulsing in response.

"Impressive," the disembodied voice sneered. "But futile. Your toys cannot harm what has already embraced the void." More guards emerged from the shadows, their forms shifting and twisting as they approached.

Elena's eyes never left the crystal orb. "We shall see," she murmured, drawing another arrow. Gloria fought valiantly beside her, her blade a silver streak in the gloom. Each time the guards attacked, Elena's arrows found their marks, sending them reeling back into the shadows from whence they came.

Aiden cornered count Aldric in the castle's highest tower, the room a whirlwind of fire and shadow. "Your reign ends here, usurper," Aiden shouted, his blade a fiery blur.

"You think you can defeat me with a child's magic?" Aldric spat, his eyes alight with dark power.

"This is no child's magic," Aiden retorted, his sword singing through the air. "This is the power of Estonia itself, the flame of rebellion that you can never extinguish!"

Their blades met with a clang that reverberated through the tower, sparks flying as they pushed each other back and forth. Aiden's fiery blade was a stark contrast to Aldric's shadowy staff, which writhed with malevolent energy. The count's eyes narrowed at the prince's words, his smile twisting into a snarl.

"You dare to challenge me?" he roared. "I have ruled over your pathetic kingdom for months, and you think you can just waltz in and take it back?"

Aiden's eyes flashed with a fire that mirrored the one dancing in his blade. "I dare because it is my birthright, and I will not stand idly by while you corrupt it with your dark arts."

"Then you will die a fool's death," Aldric sneered, casting a bolt of lightening that Aiden barely dodged.

Aiden laughed, his blade a fiery comet in the night. "I'd rather die a fool than live a monster like you!"

Their battle grew fiercer, the flaming sword and shadow staff clashing in a dance of destruction. The tower trembled as they fought, the stones of the castle seeming to shudder with each blow. Alec's tornado had reached the castle walls, setting the battlements alight and sending the skeletal soldiers reeling back.

Elena and Gloria fought back to back, the guards closing in. Despite their bravery, the shadows grew darker, and the guards more numerous. The crystal orb pulsed erratically, feeding off the chaotic magic in the room.

"Elena," Gloria shouted, her breath coming in ragged gasps, "We must hurry!"

Elena nodded, her eyes never leaving the crystal as she loosed another silver-tipped arrow. The shadows grew denser, the guards pressing closer, their forms a writhing mass of malevolence. Each time her arrow found its mark, another guard would fall, the crystal's light flickering brighter.

Outside, the fiery tornado had become a maelstrom of power, Alec's will bending the flames to his command. The skeletal soldiers were no match for the unrelenting force, their bones crumbling to dust with each fiery embrace.

In the tower, Aiden's blade sang a deadly melody, each strike a declaration of his birthright. The count's arrogant smirk began to waver, his spells becoming more erratic as Aiden's flaming sword danced closer to his heart. With a roar that seemed to shake the very foundations of the castle, Aiden launched a final, fiery assault, driving the blade through Aldric's chest. The count's eyes widened in disbelief, his mouth agape as the fire consumed him from within. His body crumpled to the floor, the shadow staff slipping from his lifeless grasp.

The room grew still, the only sound the crackling of the dying flames. Aiden stood tall, his blade still alight, his breathing heavy from the exertion of the battle. He looked down at the charred remains of the man who had stolen his throne, his heart a mix of anger and relief.

"Your reign of terror is over, Aldric," he murmured, his voice echoing through the tower. As Count Aldric breathes his last, the shadows that were dueling Elena and Gloria vanquished, and the crystal orb on the pedestal blazed with a brilliant light, as if in celebration of the usurper's defeat.

Aiden's victory cry pierced the night sky, resonating through the castle's corridors. The artifact's light grew stronger, pulsating with a newfound vitality. It was as if the castle itself was shedding its dark cloak, the very stones seeming to brighten with the promise of a new dawn.

Elena and Gloria, their eyes gleaming with triumph, turned their attention to the crystal orb. Elena raised her bow, a silver-tipped arrow poised. "For Estonia!" she shouted, and let the arrow fly. It streaked through the air, a beacon of hope in the darkness, and struck the crystal with a resounding crack. The orb shattered, the light within it exploding outwards. The room was bathed in a blinding radiance that pushed back the shadows, and the remaining guards let out a collective wail as the dark magic animating them dissipated. Their skeletal forms crumpled to the ground, lifeless once more.

The light grew brighter, a pulsing wave of power that rippled out from the tower. It flowed through the castle, down the very stones and into the ground, reaching out to the undead army that surrounded the fortress. The skeletal soldiers stumbled, their movements erratic. Alec watched in amazement as the light touched them, their bones crumbling to dust before his very eyes. The tornado of fire he had conjured faded away, no longer needed as the tide of darkness receded.

The knights cheered, their swords held high in victory. They had won the battle, but the war was far from over. Aiden's victory cry had brought hope to the people of Estonia, but the true test lay ahead. As the light reached the castle's dungeons, the siblings and their allies descended into the bowels of the castle, their hearts heavy with anticipation and fear. They had to find their father, to free him from the clutches of the dark magic that had held him captive.

The air grew thick with dust and despair as they approached the lowest level, the scent of damp stone and mildew assaulting their senses. The door to the king's cell lay ajar, and as they entered, the sight that greeted them was one of both relief and horror. King Ulric lay unconscious on the cold, stone floor, chains shackling his wrists and ankles, a crown of thorns digging into his brow. His once-regal robes were tattered, stained with grime and the residue of dark spells.

Elena's eyes filled with tears, her hand moving to her mouth to stifle a gasp. "Father," she whispered, dropping to her knees beside him. Gloria quickly moved to unshackle the king, her movements swift and practiced from her years of service to the royal family. Alec hovered over them, his magic at the ready should the need arise.

Together, they lifted King Ulric and carried him through the castle, the light from the shattered artifact guiding their way. Each step felt like a monumental victory, a declaration that the darkness was receding. The once-majestic halls were now a reminder of the horrors that had been wrought under Aldric's rule.

Elena's heart ached as she gazed upon her father, his once-noble features now a mask of pain and suffering. Despite the victory, the gravity of their task was not lost on her. They had to ensure that the true king was restored to his rightful place, that Estonia could begin to heal from the wounds inflicted by the usurper's malicious reign.

They moved him to his room, the very walls seeming to weep at the sight of their fallen monarch. The grand chamber, once a bastion of light and warmth, was now a testament to the count's cruelty, the tapestries torn and the once-shimmering mosaics marred by dark runes. Yet, as they entered, the light from the shattered artifact grew stronger, pushing back the shadows that clung to the corners.

They laid King Ulric on his bed, the softness of the pillows a stark contrast to the cold stones of his prison. Elena gently removed the crown of thorns, her eyes never leaving her father's face. His breathing was shallow and uneven, his skin pale and clammy to the touch. Alec hovered at the foot of the bed, his hands glowing with a warm, golden light as he began the delicate process of healing the king's injuries. The magic flowed from his fingertips, weaving a web of restoration that slowly mended the king's wounds.

Chapter 20:

The room grew brighter as the light from the artifact grew stronger, banishing the shadows that had clung to the corners. It was as if the very essence of Estonia was reclaiming its rightful place within the castle walls. The tapestries fluttered gently, their vibrant colors bleeding back into the fabric as the dark runes faded away. The siblings watched in awe, hope swelling in their hearts.

Aiden and Elena exchanged a solemn look. They had faced the monster that was Count Aldric and prevailed, but the true battle was only just beginning. Their father's recovery was essential to the kingdom's future, and they knew that the path ahead would be fraught with challenges. Yet, as they watched Alec's magic work its gentle miracles, they felt a renewed sense of unity and purpose.

King Ulric's eyes fluttered open, and he took a deep, shuddering breath. The siblings leaned in, their hearts racing as they watched their father's eyes focus on them. His voice, though weak and trembling, was filled with a warmth that had been absent from the castle for too long. "My children," he whispered, "I knew you would come."

Tears welled in Elena's eyes as she clutched her father's hand. "We've missed you so much," she said, her voice thick with emotion. Aiden's grip on his sword tightened, his resolve to protect his family stronger than ever.

King Ulric's gaze softened as he looked at his children. "I am so proud of you both," he murmured, his voice filled with warmth and love. "You have faced the darkness and come out stronger." He paused, taking a shallow breath before continuing, "You are the light that Estonia needs."

Elena's grip on her father's hand tightened, her eyes shimmering with unshed tears. "We will not fail you, Father," she said firmly. "We will rebuild what has been broken and restore peace to our lands."

King Ulric's smile was weak but filled with love. "I have no doubt," he murmured. "Your courage and determination have already proven that you are more than capable." He took a deep, painful breath and closed his eyes briefly, his expression one of profound relief. "Thank you, my children. For freeing me and for bringing hope back to Estonia. I'm sorry for all the pain I caused you both"

Elena's eyes widened in shock. "Father, you did no such thing," she protested. "It was Aldric's magic!"

"The damage is... irrevocable," the king rasped, his eyes filled with a deep sadness. "He has tainted my soul with his vile spells. I am afraid I cannot be restored to the man I once was."

Elena's eyes widened in shock and horror. "No," she whispered, her voice trembling. "We will find a way. We have to."

King Ulric's smile was tinged with sadness. "The dark magic Aldric used is beyond even the most powerful healers and warlocks in the land," he said softly.

Elena's eyes searched her father's, desperation clutching at her heart. "But there must be a way," she pleaded. "We can't lose you too."

King Ulric squeezed her hand, his smile a sad reflection of his former self. "The dark magic Aldric wielded was unlike any other," he said, his voice barely a whisper. "It has rooted itself deep within me, a cancer that no healer can excise." His eyes flickered to Alec, the young warlock whose magic had been instrumental in their victory. "Your power is great, Alec, but even you cannot undo this curse."

Aiden's heart clenched at his father's words. He had killed the count, but the victory felt hollow with the revelation that their father may never be the same. "What do we do?" he asked, his voice cracking.

King Ulric's eyes, though clouded by pain, bore into Aiden's. "You must rule," he said, his voice stronger than his frail body suggested. "You have the strength, the courage, and now, the support of the people. Be the king Estonia needs."

Elena's tears fell onto her father's hand as she held it tightly. "But Father, we need you," she choked out.

"The sun will rise on a new day," King Ulric whispered, his voice growing weaker. "A day when you, Aiden, will lead our people. I have faith in you, my son. And you, Elena, you will be the beacon that guides him."

Aiden's eyes grew wet, but he nodded solemnly. "I will not disappoint you, Father."

King Ulric's eyes grew dim, a heavy silence descending upon the room. "The time has come," he whispered, his breaths becoming more labored. "Before the sun rises, I will leave this world. You must be ready to lead when it does."

Elena's sobs grew louder, her heart breaking at the thought of losing her father. Aiden's jaw clenched, his eyes brimming with unshed tears as he nodded in understanding. "We will do our best, Father," he promised, his voice cracking with emotion.

King Ulric's grip tightened on their hands briefly before going slack. His eyes closed, and his chest rose and fell in shallow breaths. Alec's magic continued to flow into the king, but it was clear that the damage was too severe. The room grew quiet, the only sounds the king's labored breathing and the gentle crackle of the dying fireplace.

Elena's sobs grew quiet, replaced by a solemn determination. She wiped her tears and leaned over her father, her voice strong and clear. "We will not let your sacrifice be in vain," she whispered. "We will restore Estonia to its former glory, and we will ensure that your name is never forgotten."

Aiden nodded, his gaze never leaving his father's face. "We will be the rulers this kingdom deserves," he said, his voice echoing with the weight of his newfound responsibility.

The first light of dawn crept through the castle windows, casting a soft glow across the king's chamber. The siblings remained at their father's side, their hearts heavy with the burden of his impending departure. The room was still, the only sound the soft crackling of the fireplace and their father's labored breathing. The tapestries, once vibrant, hung lifelessly on the walls, mirroring the somber mood that had settled over them like a shroud.

Elena's eyes never left her father's face, her mind racing with the gravity of the situation. Aiden sat rigidly, his knuckles white as he clenched the hilt of his sword, a symbol of the resolve that now lay on his young shoulders. Alec stood quietly in the corner, his hands still glowing with a faint magic that had failed to revive the king. Gloria's eyes were red from crying, yet she maintained a stoic expression, her loyalty to the family unwavering even in this darkest of moments.

The first light of dawn painted the room in soft, warm hues, as if the very sun itself was trying to ease the pain of the impending loss. The shadows grew long and thin, retreating from the corners of the chamber as if in respect for the dying monarch. The air grew heavier with each of King Ulric's shallow breaths, the room a silent testament to his waning strength.

Aiden felt the weight of his father's gaze, though the king's eyes had gone unfocused. He knew that the time was near, and he gripped the hilt of his sword tighter, the warmth of the metal a comforting reminder of the promise he had made. Elena's sobs had subsided, her hand clutching their father's with a fierce determination that seemed to hold the very fabric of her being together. Gloria stood at the foot of the bed, her eyes reflecting the sorrow that filled the room, yet she remained stoic, ready to serve even in the face of such profound grief.

The first light of dawn grew stronger, Alec stepped back, his eyes glistening with unshed tears as he realized that his magic had reached its limits. The siblings exchanged a knowing glance, their hearts heavy with the understanding that the time had come to say goodbye.

King Ulric took one final, shuddering breath, and with it, the room grew colder. The light in his eyes flickered out, leaving behind an emptiness that seemed to echo through the chamber. The siblings leaned closer, their tears falling onto his lifeless hand. Aiden's hand tightened around the hilt of his sword, the metal cold against his palm. Elena's grip on their father's hand grew slack as she whispered a silent goodbye.

The castle's bell tolled mournfully, its somber echoes resonating through the halls. The funeral services had been a blur of grief and tension, a stark reminder of the battle they had won and the war they had yet to fight. Now, as the four of them stood in the throne room, the weight of their mission felt heavier than ever. The light from the shattered artifact had dimmed, leaving only the flickering torches to cast shadows across the grand chamber.

People from all across the kingdom had gathered, their faces a tapestry of hope and uncertainty. They had come to pay their respects to the fallen king and to witness the rise of a new one. The throne room, once a bastion of dark magic, had been cleansed by the light that now suffused the air. The once-shrouded windows were thrown open, allowing the sun's rays to stream in, illuminating the room with a gentle warmth. The dark runes had been scrubbed away, the very stones of the castle seeming to sigh with relief.

Aiden, clad in a cloak of royal purple, stood before the throne, his young face a mask of solemnity that belied his tender years. The crown, a heavy burden of gold and jewels, sat atop his head, the weight of his new role pressing down on his slender shoulders.

Elena, her eyes still red from crying, took her place beside him, her own grief swallowed by the fiery resolve to support her brother in the days to come. The crown was not one he had ever sought, but it was one that fate had thrust upon him, and she knew that he would bear it with honor.

Gloria stepped forward, her voice clear and strong as she announced to the hushed assembly, "With the grace of the ancients and the will of the people, I present to you, King Aiden the Brave."

Aiden, feeling the weight of his father's crown, looked out at the sea of faces before him. He was only ten, and yet here he was, the ruler of Estonia. His eyes searched the crowd for his sister, finding comfort in Elena's proud gaze. She offered a small, reassuring smile, reminding him of their pact to rule together.

He took a deep breath and turned to Alec, standing to his right. "With the power vested in me by the trust of the people," he announced, his voice echoing through the vast chamber, "I hereby appoint you, Alec as the Royal Court Warlock of Estonia."

Alec's eyes widened in astonishment. He had never expected such an honor, nor had he ever dreamed of wielding his powers openly. The young warlock stepped forward, his hand trembling slightly as he knelt before the throne. Aiden lifted the royal scepter, the orb at its tip pulsing with a gentle light. He touched it to Alec's forehead, and the boy felt a surge of warmth and acceptance flow through him.

"Rise," Aiden said solemnly, "and let your magic serve the kingdom as it has served us today." Alec stood, the weight of his new title settling upon his shoulders. He had always felt like an outsider, but now, as the Royal Court Warlock, he was part of something greater. The room erupted in a mix of applause and whispers, the people unsure of what to make of the sudden appointment of a young peasant boy to such a powerful position.

Elena stepped forward, her hand on the pommel of her sword. "And to you, my loyal subjects," she declared, her voice strong and clear, "I vow to stand beside my brother as we face the challenges ahead. Together, we will rebuild Estonia, restore peace, and honor the memory of our beloved father." The crowd's murmurs grew louder, a sense of hope kindling in their eyes as they watched the siblings stand united.

The final act of the ceremony was the lighting of the Royal Scepter, a symbol of the king's power. Alec raised his hand, and a small flame danced upon his fingertip. He touched it to the crystal orb, and the room grew brighter as the light grew, filling the chamber with a warm, golden glow that seemed to resonate with the heart of the kingdom itself. The scepter blazed with power, and Aiden took it in his hands, feeling its energy thrumming through him.

With a heavy heart, he took his seat on the throne, his sister beside him. The room grew silent, the weight of the moment palpable. Alec stepped back, his eyes shimmering with unshed tears, as the siblings faced the assembly. The sun had fully risen outside, its light spilling in through the windows, a promise of a new day for Estonia.

Don't miss out!

Visit the website below and you can sign up to receive emails whenever Art Vulcan publishes a new book. There's no charge and no obligation.

https://books2read.com/r/B-A-MJTMC-WFLBF

BOOKS 2 READ

Connecting independent readers to independent writers.

Milton Keynes UK
Ingram Content Group UK Ltd.
UKHW040255181024
449757UK00001B/26